I0831414

THE SEASTEADERS

The Seasteaders

SHEL GRAVES

ISBN: 979-8-9985486-2-8

First Printing, 2025 Sheltopian Press

CONTENTS

This book is dedicated to the Underdark Calligraphy Club — and to my beloved Sam.

PROLOGUE

While I am swimming, I think of what I have learned. I think of love. Love crosses distances. It expands across miles, across continents, across barriers of soul or sea. Distance does not break or dissolve love. I have loved from under oceans and come to love from beyond my body. My capacity to love is boundless and boundaryless and it is the strongest part of my aspect. Yes, I admit, I have been slow to learn love's lessons. In my first life, I was slow to love and learn. I was slow to understand our capacity for transformation. I never met Geneva Weltraum who transformed our thoughts. I was never psychic. I never knew Doreena Flora Moriena who changed our being. I never knew the liquid island of her love. Yet, those who went before me, my mothers and sisters of transformation, loved me. They were the waves of my life. Still, before I met the Mulians, I did not even think much of the capacity of love, its ancestral underwater nature. Afterwards, the stretch and reach of love became my obsession. Earlier in life, I did not think of love at all. Later, thoughts of love consumed me.

Watch me now swim to land. I reach a distant shore tired but ready to share my message at last. I begin to hum my song as I approach the land and prepare to speak.

"Love you. Appreciate you. Thank you," I say with shallow breaths when I first pull myself out of the water. "I see you and, of course, I know you."

This is how I always begin the conversation with the first person I encounter on shore--this time, a boy. I raise myself half out of the water. I am still wet with sea. While he is statuesque with shock, I say what is important before the chance slips away. I have to be direct, to assure these people of my humanity.

I was human once although I do not look it now. Sometimes the land people run away and sometimes they stay to listen; it depends upon the person.

This boy has stopped in curiosity, but my first words have scared him. He is old enough that people rarely say they love him outright anymore and too young to be thanked. He could be a young General Balor.

"I am not a monster," I tell him. "I was a child once, a person, an ordinary lander, just like you."

He points at my bare breasts, and I laugh at the absurdity that these body parts might still be the most startling thing about me.

"Oh, yes, but I was a little girl."

I wish the people could see past my appearance immediately, but it takes time. I've swum many miles through the Rust Sea. I have wrinkles and barnacles that twist across my rust red skin to horrific effect, but deep in my scars there is beauty, too--lavender, cerulean, and sea green pearlescent droplets and rivulets like an oyster shell. I hoist myself out of the water to bare it all--my twisted beauty still becoming.

If these people are willing to listen, I will have to tell the entire story so that they can understand. We are in a hurry for the waters are quickly rising, but the story can't be rushed. For decades our people have been warring on opposite isles of Pacifica over pinnacles of land. Even Sync Chrome City's psychics and Mirror Island's surfers could not stop the hatred. Perhaps Geneva should not have befriended Burrows. Perhaps Doreena should have preserved the island and not let herself become so diluted. But, motivated by loves, what choice did they have? So, the killing went on for centuries while the waves rose. We prayed for mercy, ineffectually, then stopped. It is hard to have faith in anything solid while the land slips away from under our feet.

I am here to offer a liquid solution.

I wish the landed people could just see the truth of what I am about to tell them in my eyes. In truth, though, my soul looks untrustworthy, piratical. I have the look of an Elathian Riptider. It's the way the lines have set about my eyes--a tangled combination of fear, tragedy, saltwater, wind, sun, and laughter. There's nothing reliable or settled-looking about me. I have aged into this beautiful, twisted sea wrecked shape.

I've gone where I was pulled, lived as I had to, leapt when it was demanded and left the ones I love. After I tell my story, I'll leave these people too. This is my truth may it be one of many: While others clung to the land, I departed for the sea. I went because the Mu offered peace, which I covet, having experienced none in this lifetime. There was also the offer of breath—of survival. Just that can turn the tides of fate. Just that. Just.

I follow the boy to his village where I'll place my hand upon the speaking staff, because these people have learned that lesson how to let each other speak. I wrap my webbed fingers around the smooth red Madrona wood and I tell the story I have come to tell in the public square. My real story, however, began below, as all stories will one day, in a place robbed of breath.

The villagers gather. They appear breathless. They wait for me to begin.

"I want to take you down with me under the Salish Sea," I do not say.

"I do not want to go alone or be alone ever again," I do not say.

It hurts to hold in these words. It is like drowning and at the same time I am euphoric. I sacrifice my own desires again and again to save my world, to help my people. There is no doubt that this is what I do.

The little boy who brought me before the rest of his people reminds me, too much, of General Balor. It's in the set of his lip and in his bravery.

I remember watching the old man die and how I did not move to save him.

He could have been a good man, the general, as much as any of us. The Mu have taught me that. I feel the shame of my inaction. I feel my guilt. Still, I must come before these people as a savior. They will have to save themselves, but first they must believe me. I will keep my faults and my crimes to myself. So, in this way, it is fortunate the psychics never crossed the water. It was meant to be. The world works as the waters flow.

I begin by telling these people about my first ratfin, pet. They can all relate to a child's love for a pet. The people, themselves, always remind me of ratfin -- with their squirminess, their fear, and their resistance.

Then, I tell them about my mother's bruises. These people understand that, too. They know full well the depths of war and pain.

One of the things the Mu taught us Seasteaders was a different sense of time, but even so I feel as though I am talking forever. Time rides differently on the land. I'm growing impatient. The waters are rising.

At least the story is spreading--these landers nod when I speak as though they have heard parts of this tale before. It does not strike them as entirely fantastical. It's somewhat familiar. Our plan begins to change the tides.

I, and my lovers, have been swimming and swimming and sharing our story. I hope this village tells the next one and the next one and on and on--in time this truth becomes easier to believe. The myth spreads and becomes reality.

When everyone knows and is ready to go underwater, I can be with my lovers again. Hope hurts, but I can be patient. I anticipate our reunion in salt and sea.

"The acidic water is rising," I tell the boy. "You must learn to swim in it."

I look out at the crowd.

"It could take a lifetime to rebuild the road to Mu. But please, please, consider (my love, my dear, my darling: I do not say) they'd give you more than one to do it."

Part One: Love

~ 1 ~

LEAVING HOME

Clean, bright, washed by time, like a dirty stone plunged under a sunlit stream, the bruises on mother's cheeks and her blade-scarred forearms--the bright purple and red swatches of skin--look beautiful in my memory.

There was nothing clear or beautiful about her scars though when I standing in front of them at age seven, eye level. When I received the first coin to Mu, I was horrified.

Everything around us was a scramble.

"Hurry, Nata!" my mother called.

Her bags were lined up in the hall with everything packed. I had refused to pack my carpetbag because I didn't understand where were going. I was afraid of this change.

"I can't," I said. "I don't know what to take."

Mother said there wasn't room for everything. She pulled me into my room. My bag was open on my bed. She pulled clothes from the dresser and flung them into it.

"It doesn't matter," she said.

We had moved before, many times, inland, everyone did as the waters rose, but always before things had been important: meticulously packed and tucked into tight packages that must be carried gently and positioned into the kowal drawn cart. There was hardly room for all those things, but we had carted them carefully from the house on Salish Island when we'd left it for Orcas: when my father lost his job, after the factory flooded, and the soldiers wanted our house on the hill.

My mother had been so cautious about those things: the vase given to her by Aunt Virgie, the doilies made by cousin Tolly, the ceramic figures collected by cousin Shad. Now those same items were ignored, left high on shelves I could not reach.

Father had gone to the grocery. Mother made some excuse for why she could not go. He had had a craving for eel, so he had gone himself. I do not know why she picked that time. It was not enough time, the grocery was quite near, but it must have seemed sufficient. The wait for a lover's return is the slow ingress of a tide, but the flight from a lover is a tsunami. While we were standing there with our bags mostly packed, mother consulted her seeing shells. Somehow there was time for that?

She shook the little felt bag, reached in for one shell piece, and examined its upturned jagged edges.

"We have everything. We're ready to go," she finally said. Then, "I don't know if I can do this."

She sounded frantic. My mother had been with my father for eight years.

The rest of shells rattled in her hand. Then stopped as she closed her fist tight around them. It must have hurt. She dropped the bag and the shells scattered across the bamboo floor.

"Grab your bag," she said, staring at a piece of upturned coral.

She left the shards laying in the entryway for father to see, or more likely to step on and grind into powder. He did not believe in portents, would not be calmed by the shells, and would not agree with our departure no matter what they said.

The objects I left were dolls, ceramic figurines, and the jewelry box with the spinning dolphin inside. Things had to be left so father wouldn't suspect right away that we were gone for good, so that he wouldn't try to follow.

I cried over these things in a torrent on that day and it was really the loss of those small objects that disturbed me most. I didn't understand what loss meant, then. For a long time after that, I refused to cry over things. Looking back, that moment severed my attachment to objects. I lost my most precious things and then everything solid became unimportant. I never let myself love another material good. I tucked my capacity for love away inside. I hid it inside a thickening shell.

My mother never understood this. For her, each new item she obtained became all the more precious as it represented that which was lost.

In Mu, I learned a different way to think about objects and gained an appreciation for my mother's perspective. I understood her better after living with the Mulians. For her, all those objects had souls. They connected her to people I couldn't picture in faraway places, on islands that she would never reach again, on lands that might no longer exist above the sea.

At the time though, I saw only her foolishness, her excess, a kind of greed and focus on goods that didn't matter. I could only love ideas, the ethereal, which could not be broken or left behind, so I mistakenly thought. Mother loved her things, but if we took them, father would know we meant to leave him forever.

How to leave things wasn't a lesson my mother needed to learn in that lifetime, unfortunately. She didn't gain anything by it. Loss of beloved things was just something she suffered, another source of pain. We had to travel light.

For me, it was different: It was my time to absorb this meaning. This was the beginning of how I learned lightness.

In Mu, they believed that every object had a soul. They would no more purposefully destroy a vase than they would shatter a person's body. This made them cautious about how many objects they took into their care. They felt a responsibility for things throughout their lives and they passed on that responsibility carefully. This did not make them less reverent of Mulian life; it made them more so. Someone who cares for silent, stoic shells is even more careful with a Mulian being they can hear breathing.

In Mu, I learned that in my past life, in many lives, I hoarded objects, so in this lifetime I'm asked to learn to let go. Pacifica, in the time of the Rust Sea when everything was floating or corroding away, was a perfect place for my rebirth. I often had to remind myself that it was a blessing, truly, how thoroughly I was learning this lesson.

With the Rust Sea rising, Pacifica's islands were shrinking. Gradually, everyone had to learn to let go. For me, it was like an amputation, when my mother's flight removed me from home in one fell swoop. As a child this blessing was misery.

I took comfort in one thing: my ratfin pet, Ea.

My mother hurried me, but I wouldn't leave without Ea. I wasn't crying over this though. Instead, I put his water dish into the cage, covered it with a towel and yanked it off the shelf. Tears take over in times when there is nothing. When there remains room for action, there are no tears. When the water is rising and there is nothing to be done but drown, then it is time to cry and join the ocean in sympathy. Much later, when I left my twin soul Georgios, I jumped into the ocean and cried because there was nothing else to be done.

Then, as a child, my eyes were dry and focused. From this distance, however, many years and losses later, it was impossible not to feel sympathy for the shaken ratfin. It looked like a toy of soaked, jumbled grey fur and fin under that towel.

I picked up the cage and mother dropped my hand to fill her other hand with carpetbag handles. Mother had the most beautiful hands and I had always hoped to inherit them. Instead, in the watery way of fate, I would grow webbed fingers.

"Nata," mother said, stepping over the seeing shells to open the door to the apartment. She swung her carpetbag at the door and ushered me ahead of her. The apartment, as we left it, looked the same as it ever had except the life had gone out of the carefully arranged objects within it: vases, doilies, woodcarvings (grandmother was quite wealthy), and ceramic figurines. I held onto Ea's cage and made my mother carry everything else. She managed to take my own bag as well. I later learned that to do this she'd had to leave behind one of her own bags. It was the one with her suits in it. Later, she'd had to beg for work clothes.

Once outside, I was terrified. I was afraid of the street, the wagons and the big, hairy kowals that pulled them. I thought we would get hit standing there on the street or shat on. I worried about my father. He could have come at any time. Why had he taken so long? Had he been deterred by soldiers at the grocery? Forced conscription into General Balor's army was always a fear. Why hadn't he gotten back in time to stop us so I could be back in my pale blue bedroom? My room in the old house had been blue and they'd stained the new one in town in the apartment a light blue, too. It was a last luxury. They didn't want me to feel uprooted, so I tried not to. That was the kind of child I was, pliant as kelp.

There was a carriage waiting for us outside.

"Please, wait. We're coming," my mother said.

The driver frowned at the cage. He looked pensive and ready to leave. You could see he was sorry he'd accepted this fare, at this time of the night, and in this part of the war-torn city. We piled in and I put the cage on my lap. The kowals splashed through the soggy streets. I peered under the cloth to see Ea's whiskered little nose dripping.

"Hurry, now," he said. "It's been a soggy day."

"You know," mother said, turning to me. "It was your father's idea to get you that ratfin."

It was true. Father had a strange sense of humor, strange ideas about how to raise his only child. He didn't want me to be like anyone else. He was right, no one else I knew kept ratfin, but then I didn't know many other children. The next time I met someone who kept a ratfin for a pet I'd be an adult and the ratfin keeper would be a Riptider.

What struck me in mother's comment was her tone of disdain, a sound of separation that I'd never heard from her before. The Mulians lived long lives, many hundreds of years, and even then, they did not believe we end at death. We come and go like the tides, they said. We return with fresh lessons to cast upon the sands. There are new objects we are meant to pick up or leave: a sand dollar, a piece of kelp, a creature's body, or its calcium husk. My mother's lessons to relearn in that lifetime were: how to leave a lover and that people do not always tell the truth.

My parents didn't have many friends. They lost their first mates in the 100 Island Wars, and then kept new ones away with their private war. Maybe that's why my father wanted me to have the ratfin. They were both pacifists, who had refused to fight, which is ironic because they fought so much at home. They had relatives on other isles of Pacifica, but the war came home to us anyway.

We never lived in isolation. Even on islands, our culture came home to us. Culture surrounded us like a sea, and we were cast about in it subject to its violence or its calms. This is why I wanted so much to create a condition of peace, to find a new way.

I never considered myself to be a victim of violence because father never hit me. Mother took the blows, and they went around me. When they fought, I didn't exist. Our house was too small for me to be safe in my room, so I would slip from home with Ea in my pocket. I went to the estuary downhill from our house. In the weedy tall grasses, I sat watching the still water.

In fall, when the weather turned, my mother gave me a coat made of trumpeter feathers. It was twice the size of other kids' coats, and it could have kept Far North explorers warm. It wasn't an attractive coat, but the mottled black-green color made it perfect camouflage for hiding in the estuary at dusk. It smelled of marsh and cattails. Other kids lost their coats or whined about wearing them, but I always had mine. I took it with me when I escaped from the house, while my parents waged their private war. I imagined my mother had given the coat to me for just this purpose. She expected me to abandon her. This was where I learned to leave the ones I love in times of stress, a shameful skill I have used over and over again.

Wrapped in my coat, I would go to the water even in the winter on days when ice crisped the marsh's edges and the pampas and cattails gleamed with a coat of hoar frost. I would go even at night when I could only see the water as a glimmer, a reflection of the moon. Even in the snow, I put my coat on and went out to my safe place.

The first time that I remember my parents fought, I thought guiltily of how I had left my mother, back there, alone. I imagined her hurts. I pictured her dying. I sat on a damp stone with my feet planted on muddy earth and cried. I dripped wet tears onto Ea whose fur and scales already looked gleaming black, wet, and shiny. Ea placed his webbed paws on my chest. With repetition, though, I became accustomed to the pattern of my parents' private war. I did not imagine I had any control over these fights or could help mother in any way. It wasn't just my youth that made me passive.

I had been swept into my culture and floated with it on the outer winds of Pacifica. We were all caught up in wars and rising waters. I had not yet considered another way and it did not seem necessary to consider a course of action. My mother had bruises and tears, but she remained. My father was distant, but that was usual unless he was cheerily bringing home presents--ceramic kowal figurines for me and gold and silver bangles for my mother. Many of the necklaces and bracelets he gave her were handmade from his forge. These were his talents: battery, handcrafts, and lying. One of these I learned from him.

I learned that if I waited long enough, if I became engrossed in play, when I returned the table would be bright and filled with wet, nutrient foods--bok choy, water chestnuts, and water cabbages--and my mother would have already dabbed chamomile lotion on her bruises. This was how I became good at imagining and developed my philosophy that if you dream hard enough, you can make the world a better place--or ignore its faults, anyway. I hadn't yet learned to put my dreams into action.

In that estuary, I began my life's work again. Lifetime after lifetime, I had sought to attain what I would finally achieve in this one--so it came to me young. I knew my purpose. I saw the patterns in the world like my mother saw them in her seeing shells: ripples in the pond, flowing grasses, and fractals of leaves. I imagined arranging my world in the way my mother arranged plates and knives and napkins and dishes of rice, bean sprouts, watercress, and bamboo shoots, to realign our family. Of course, at that age, the wide world with its wars over the remaining peaks of islands was too much for me to imagine. Instead, I imagined my own small dominion. I called my invented paradise Octavia.

On that estuary, lived my imagined wee Octavian people.

They would build a colony, a tiny walled fortress while, I, an all-powerful, omniscient giantess watched over them and ordered their lives. One brave Octavian hero would be called to ride the giant ratfin back to the house for food. It would take two days at least depending on what they encountered (a fox or hawk). They'd risk everything for a dab of my mother's rice pudding, which would last the Octavian people weeks.

My imaginary land Octavia wasn't messy, disorganized, drowning, or war torn. The branches that made the city were laid neatly parallel. The people made the most of what they needed themselves. The trips to the house were merely a luxury. Octavians never fought. No one shouted or dominated. They held reasoned discussions and dissenters were cast out and, therefore, eaten by insects and vermin.

Sometimes, I would be so involved with Octavia that my mother would have to come out to the estuary to fetch me. She'd bring me in for a late dinner when the fight had passed and it was time to indulge in reunion food, a stew of vegetable gumbo.

Of course, reality, and the brutality of my home, could not always be ignored. Once I returned to the house after dark and found it empty. When my parents returned, my mother's arm was bandaged in a sling, and they avoided each other's eyes.

"I don't think he believed you," my father said holding the apothecary bottle while my mother bent over the cutting board and then laid out the thick stone plates with her one good hand.

Another time, the soldiers came across the fields riding clanging metal-draped kowals, stupidly impractical for those water-laden times. General Balor's advantage was his viciousness, not his forethought. Mother brought me inside then. I heard father yelling in the front yard. Then, I heard the thump of a man falling--and silence. Father returned bruised and dirty. Bested. I thought it served him right; until much later when I had quenched my thirst for revenge.

How dare father yell at those metal-plated men the way he yelled at mother? Later, I respected him in a way--at least he treated everyone alike. There was honesty to his impulsive violence. He could not control himself for anyone.

"General Balor says his troops need this high ground," my father said.

Not long after that, we left the house on Salish Island and moved to smaller Orcas Island and into town. I remember little of the journey, but it was not by boat. Back then there were still a few bridges.

My father told me the origin of the island's name. Of course, he was a fabulous storyteller.

"Orcas were a kind of whale, black and white, with sharp teeth. They were among the first animals killed by the corrosion leaching into the sea. They were sensitive creatures," he said. "Not like your mother."

This was a dig at mother's heritage. She was an Iron Blood and from that, proudly, she said she gained her toughness. My father turned it into an insult and punished her for it.

Fortunately for us, it was not possible to identify the Iron Bloods by appearance. Some blamed my mother's people for the rust entering the sea--as if the blood General Balor's soldiers had spilled into it were a pollutant. It was true that my mother's people--the Iron Bloods--had a tradition of bloodletting at sea as part of their burial rites. In the old days, when there were orcas, it was considered a great honor if one's body were snatched, shaken, and consumed by one of the whales.

Iron Blood was why the seas were growing red and poisonous, liars said. It was true when I licked my own blood, it tasted like the Rust Sea, but it did not sicken me. I even let Ea lick one of my wounds once, when I cut my finger on a shell, but he did not sicken, either. I did not think my blood was poison.

When we left again, the apartment this time, only my mother and I; my mother took all her jewelry. She sat in that carriage with gold bands up to her elbows and her neck weighed down by chains.

"Where to, mum?" the driver asked.

"To pawn," my mother said.

The driver drove us to the pawnbroker. It was the first time I'd been to such a shop. There were bars on the windows. Inside, it smelled of damp and muddled loss. There were few items, and most were what was left behind when homes were flooded, and people moved to higher ground.

It was at once a frightening and intriguing place. There were guns and wooden oars on the walls and tricycles on the floor: children's toys mingled with adult ones on the shelves. There were knives under the counter of all types: rusted bowies, thick hunting wedges, and long, sleek blades. There were sparkling gold rings and black, gold, and pink pearls.

We were in the pawnshop a long time, it seemed. It was a place to lose time in and a place to get lost. Was my mother hesitating? I do not know.

"It used to be all women had was jewelry, what was given, and what they could wear. I never liked all this," my mother said as she unloaded her gold onto the counter. "It's blood money. People die to mine gold and dive for pearls. It's an evil. Your father never understood how I felt, how it stung, when he gave me these things by way of apology. All this added insult, burden, and ache. It feels good to be done with it."

Mother understood instinctively, with Mulian clarity, how objects could be a burden, how they must be carried from place to place and cared for like children to survive the chaos of these times.

I watched the man behind the counter grin. He was glad to take the weight. You could see she'd spoken too much in front of him to make a good bargain.

"Happy to be of service," he said, without a trace of deference.

I didn't tell her that father had given me a jewel too, after one of their fights. It was a small pearl strung on a steel chain. Its black surface reflected purple waves in swirls of silver and green. I could not have imagined then that one day my skin would look like that. I could not imagine that one day I would be pearling.

The color was unique. I didn't think mother had one like it. Father had told me not to tell her about the gift, and I hadn't. I knew she wouldn't have liked that he had given it to me. I wasn't sure I liked receiving it myself. It felt dangerous and secret. I well knew what came with these kinds of surprises. It was the black-purple of a bruise, but it was such a pretty, small thing. I could not have refused. Now I took it out from under my shirt and released the clasp. I laid it on top of her pile of gold. It sparkled there. I wanted Mother to know I understood her lesson. She looked at me and began to cry.

"I was right to leave," she said. "I was right." As if, until that moment, there had yet been some doubt in her. Father's lies sunk deep.

There, in the pawnshop, while my mother and the clerk haggled I discovered the medallions. I looked under the case at all the gold discs. I vaguely understood the concept of pawning. The shop was filled with things stolen or lost because of poverty and fear or things abandoned as the water rose that people were glad to lose or could not take. Meaningless currency was got in return.

The medallions though, were money, given in exchange for money, and displayed as though they had greater value than the stuff kept in your pocket. It was confusing. Why? I thought they must be a kind of magic. Maybe an ill kind. I knew soldiers received them in exchange for deeds done in battle. There were special medallions given for killing Iron Bloods.

My mother, though, was not enchanted by anything in this place. It repelled her, but she lingered. Did she hope Father would find us?

She was still under father's spell--although it was seeping away.

"I never cared about those things. Just like you never cared about those toy kowals," she said.

When they'd made the deal, the man looked up startled when he saw the name on the chit and he counted the money out slowly. It made my mother nervous. She held out her hand for the coins, "What's wrong?"

She'd been tense for trouble and now she was sure this was the beginning of it. My Father was a brilliant player at card games, especially Cardinal. He was a wicked strategist--something good he gave me. He often had a trump card and now she thought this was the playing of it, some way he'd anticipated her and blocked our retreat.

"You Nata Lang?" the broker said.

My mother remained silent and glared at him, but I said, "I am." Defiantly.

Mother turned her glare on me.

"He says I'm s'posed to give you...a thing," he hesitated.

"No, we don't want anything. Just the cash," mother said. In a place like this, that should have been obvious.

"It's no mind. It's naught, but for the little 'un."

This angered me. I never thought of myself as small. In my imagination I was a giantess, the great leader of an organized society--a mighty Octavian.

He held out the coin to me, the first I received. "Take it now. No fuss. I'm s'posed to give it you." He looked at my mother. "Or I cain't give you the cash. I don't want no trouble, not of that kind, no."

My mother nudged me. "Hurry then."

I held out my hand and he dropped the coin onto it. I didn't examine it then, just noticed it was cool and light and gold. It flickered in my palm like a fish scale.

"From father?" I asked, and watched as the man spun his rings round his fingers and looked at me askance.

He scoffed, "Only if'n your a fish."

My mother got her cash and we went back to the carriage. "Take us to the dock," she said to the driver.

I put the coin in my pocket and we boarded the last night ferry to La Merde where my grandmother lived.

"It's not just me. Eventually, he would have hurt you too. I got you out just in time," mother said.

No matter that I knew it was true, I wished mother wouldn't speak truths to me so unsparingly. I didn't want to hear so plainly how father could hurt me. I see now, I've inherited her trait of blunt talk.

Mother alternated between rage and tears. She took a letter from her pocket and wept over it. Really, she wasn't thinking of me at all. Mother was still thinking about Father and so was I. We were leaving him. So I left her too, and wandered to roam the deck of the boat.

It smelled of wet metal and rust. In the moonshine, rust speckled the waves as we rode. I realized how long it had been since I'd been beside so much water. Once we'd moved to town, I'd had nowhere to run to during their fights. I'd hid in my room, but even there I was surrounded. The rooms shook and I waited for the day when my bedroom door would open, and their terror would turn on me. Now the sea spray felt so fine on my face--no matter that it tasted like rust and left my skin red and chaffed--I imagined my city of Octavia and the little people riding the waves. This was where the little people longed to be. Living on the estuary, they'd been refugees. This was the Octavian's true home, on the sea, I imagined. Some monster had made them leave it. On the ocean at night, I felt peace for the first time since our move away from the house by the estuary, my pale blue bedroom, and my marshland.

While I was standing on the deck, I took ratfin out of his cage. It seemed to me he was sluggish as I warmed him in my hands and then held him over the railing to peer down at the murk passing beneath us. I felt him shivering and pulled him close to my chest unbuttoning my jacket so he could snuggle there. Then he gasped twice and went still. There was no mistaking the departure of his soul, the sudden emptiness of his body in my hands, heavy and dead. I don't know if it was from the stress, the cold, old age or if I'd clutched him too tightly too my chest--all of these possibilities crossed my mind--either way Ea was still and stiff. My ratfin friend was dead.

Only his whiskers and fins trembled, shaking in my upheld hand. I was startled, more than anything, by my first encounter with death. It was sudden, but so much less violent than the life I was used to. I was drawn to the peacefulness in that still body. If I had known the word I would have said "transcendent". I looked at ratfin's body and wondered, "Where has he gone?" As I held him in my hands, I saw perfect stillness. Only the rumbling of the ferry disturbed him. I had the sense that he had gone somewhere. I was curious. I wanted to follow him into that space, that stillness. I wanted to explore it, as I have always wanted to explore everything. I have always been unable to leave things alone--death least of all.

The next thing I did was hold him over the railing and drop him into the sea below. The body disappeared in the night. I imagined it tumbled into the rust waves. Is this shocking and strange? Well, it startled me too what I did.

It seemed the right thing to do at the time: an Iron Blood burial at sea. It came to me naturally. In the next moment, I panicked. I thought after I did this, that I'd made a mistake: That he wasn't dead, and I had killed him. He'd wake up in the water and swim, corrode, and freeze to death, dying from exhaustion or cold. The thought has haunted me ever since. I am usually at home in the water, but when I am afraid this is why. It's not the corrosion I fear; it's the scraping fins, the wheezing whiskers, the ratfin ghosts.

I covered the cage and ran across the deck seeking the comfort of my mother's arms.

That's when the ferry broke down. It came to a grinding halt as often happened in those days. The crew began to shout and mother came rushing out onto to the deck. She grabbed me and tightened my life vest. The rusty, creaky old boat could sink. The sea and the acid billows in it were corroding the metal. I bawled on mother's shoulder, but as I had reason enough to do so, she didn't question me. She assumed my reasons were the same as hers, and she hugged me to offer comfort. I think, too, she had tired of nursing her own grief. I was a welcome distraction for once.

Eventually, they got the ferry engine going again and we landed in La Merde the next morning. I never told my mother how I'd dumped Ea into the sea. I never got around to it. She never asked after it. I just fingered the coin in my pocket and tried not to imagine my ratfin, my mother, my father, and me submerged in those rusty, murky, churning depths.

~ 2 ~

LA MERDE

More than any other placed I had lived, La Merde smelled of fish and rust. The town went uphill from the ferry dock. Up was the only way to go on that mountain island. The land, when we stepped off ship, squished beneath our boots--a bad omen for the town. Even at that age, the sponginess under my feet made me anxious. In my teens, it would terrify me. Then, as an adult, it would inspire me. Later, it meant nothing, nothing. The drowning of the land meant nothing to me at all.

The sun rose as mother and I walked up the cobblestone to my grandmother's house. La Merde was bustling with townsmen, and although the town was not yet overrun with General Balor's soldiers, several men with bayonets marched along the streets. I did not then notice the pale-yellow ornamented buildings with their arches and turrets--except to note that it was a pretty town. Later, though, I would be preoccupied with La Merde's low-lying university. I did note the round dome of the Iron Blood Church. Its blue color pleasantly reminded me of my painted bedroom at home. It was shocking though to see the words Iron Blood in public. That place augured loss and sadness.

When we passed through the town and veered West up the hill, I was startled to see the red and green street placard naming the winding road ahead. It read Octavia Street--the name of my fantasy town. This seemed magical to me and poignant. The obvious, that I'd once seen the name written on letters when I was young and had co-opted it for my fantasy adventures, did not occur to me. As a babe, I had been here before.

My grandmother met us at the end of the walkway. She was thinner even than my mother and pale in a long dark dress. My mother looked surprised to see her standing there beside the tuberoses lining the walk. She'd been given to think my grandmother was bedridden. This looked not to be the case, although on our slow walk into the house, I had plenty of time of observe the overgrown gardens and the tangled roses surrounding the house.

From what I'd heard of my grandmother, this wildness was not her usual way. She was ill in some way and worse, she was lonely, and too tired to maintain her formal gardens. Later, I would find sketches of what the gardens had been when grandfather had been alive. While he'd spent time teaching and researching at the university, she'd created mazes of hedges and lined the rows with blossoms. Nearly all of it was edible. I inherited some of my bent for planning, conspiracy, and design from grandmother. She had been a meticulous, practical woman, but she, too, was learning to let things go.

The house was a mansion with two long wings. There were thorny brambles everywhere arching over the stone path and dropping half-ripe berries onto it. Vines snaked up the second story. Gnarled trees, by a trick of perspective, poked through the mossy angled roof. I had never lived in a house like this. On Salish we had lived in a mud hut with a grass roof dug into the side of a hill. It was warm and clean, though sometimes damp and wormy, but there were just a few rooms: the kitchen and bedrooms. Our apartment on Orcas was two rooms with a bamboo floor. I slept in the living area. The building was cobbled together of thatch. Grandmother's house, Tillitat Manor, was stone--and there were many, many rooms.

Inside, it smelled of anise, rosewood, and citrus. It was a mixture of the orange-scented oil grandmother used to polish her banisters and tables, the handmade rose lotion grandmother slathered on each morning, and her favorite persimmon tea from Hattie's stall in the market. The house was crammed with doilies as though the ones we'd had at home had flown here and bred. The ceramic animals had been active, too, displayed in all the nooks. The downstairs was an enormous living room and kitchen.

I don't remember much else of that first day except my mother and grandmother talking in low muffled voices. I was too tired even to eavesdrop. My mother led me upstairs to sleep. At the top of the stairs with the elegant wooden banister, I stood stock still, amazed. The long hallway stretched in either direction. There were doors and doors and rooms and rooms down the East wing and the West.

I left footprints down the dust-covered floorboards as I walked to the master bedroom. The room had been grandmother's and untouched since she'd moved downstairs. It was painted a cool blue like the roof of the Iron Blood Church. The window looked up Octavia Street where the cobblestone path steepened and narrowed. That tangle at the top was the marketplace. Mother left me. My matriarchs had plans to discuss, and I would hear their voices rising from the kitchen long into that first night. Even exhausted, it was hard to sleep in that strange new place.

The closet was filled with dark clothes permeated with a rose scent. There were mourning outfits of black boots, lace handkerchiefs, silk gloves, black crepe trousers, and dresses. Since grandfather's death and his sea-fairing funeral and her steady decline, grandmother stayed on the first floor in a smaller, warmer room behind the kitchen. She'd made that concession to infirmity. It could have been a maid's quarters, but my grandparents, even in that mansion, had never had servants.

"We are all family. You pay someone, that puts them beneath you," grandmother often said. But I had the feeling she thought someone should have helped her keep house without being asked or paid. That someone should have been mother, and perhaps myself. "We're Iron Bloods. We stick together."

There it was again the words Iron Blood spoken open as sky here in the shelter of the blue dome of their church. Grandmother did not shrink from her heritage or hide it.

Mother and I settled distractedly into the house, and it was some time before she commented on my ratfin's absence. While we were busy caring for grandmother and soothing my mother's wounded heart, many things went unnoticed--like the arrival of General Balor and the sinking of the grounds around the university. The cobbled streets by the ferry dock were growing rust red with the telltale algae--the only life that thrived in the toxic slime--moist gunk carried off the boat on the boots of the soldiers and steadily uphill. I later learned that grandmother's illness, her need for a nurse, was part of what had convinced my mother to leave father. Grandmother healed rapidly from that first feigned illness. She was no more in need of cosseting than any other elderly widow.

When mother finally did remark on ratfin's absence, I lied. "I lost him during the move," I said. "He escaped his cage."

I wanted Ea's death and his ferry sea-fairing to be my secret.

La Merde was strangely peaceful as the war was building. Balor's soldiers were recruiting from other isles and their numbers were growing, but there was no one to fight, as yet. In those early days, it was so pleasant. I wondered why we had not crossed the sea sooner. I soon found out.

"It was your father," grandmother said. "He preferred the war to the threat of my frail person."

That was true, but not the whole truth. Father had other reasons not to want us near our blood kin. In some respects, he had been right. It had been safer for me and my mother to be far away from the other Iron Bloods. On Salish Island and on Orcas, mother and I blended in. Few people on outlying isles were attuned to thinking about blood. Who cared what flowed beneath the surface of the skin? Besides, Iron Bloods kept to their own. On La Merde, surrounded by kin, we were targets. Balor's men knew where to find us.

Father never did come after us. Ferries ran infrequently between the islands and the threat of conscription likely kept him away.

That first year, he sent letters that made my mother cry.

"He says he loves you," she said.

I often heard her arguing with my grandmother after those letters came. In the aftermath, grandmother would often fall ill again. Her health seemed fragile. We'd become busy at her beck and call bringing watercress soup, tuberose poultices, and anise teas.

Later on, the letters stopped and so did the tears.

I imagined father now yelled at another woman with another little girl. He gave them pearls and his hand-carved kowals. They lined the walls of my replacement's blue room.

To make myself at home in grandmother's house, I looked for water. From the attic, a triangle of purple-red ocean was just visible perched over the thatch of neighboring rooftops between the vine-laced trees. This vantage also afforded a clear view of the steady stream of men and women leaning into the hill as they climbed toward the rising tower of smoke at the height of La Merde--the hubbub of the market where they sold smoked fish and dried herbs. For someone else, this attic might have been the perfect sanctuary, but for me it was far too confined.

I found my place when I went out to look for my next ratfin. Mother agreed I could replace my pet and grandmother often sent me out to buy her teas and the oils she needed for her lotions. Like most people, we grew the majority of our groceries, but there were a few luxuries and exotic fruits for sale in the market. I followed the line of pilgrims walking up the winding road to the cobblestone market at the end of Octavia Street. It smelled of damp algae air, mulling spices, and curry. The goods at the market center were mostly cloths and food stuffs, but I found an old woman with a pen of ratfin beside the canal. I negotiated a price with her, doing my best to bargain, but unnerved by the way she squinted at me with her red eyes as if taking an accounting of my soul. Then, when I went for my purse, I found I was shy a few coin.

"Ah sure, you are. You're wastin' my time then," she said.

I had already chosen my ratfin from among them. She was a limber beast with especially lacy, dark, torn-looking fins. I could already feel her curled at the corner of my neck where I would train her to ride. Disappointed, I turned away, but then I remembered the gold coin from the pawnbroker. I unbuttoned the small pocket by my breast.

"And this!" I said triumphantly, laying it in the palm of the woman's hand.

"Wot's this?" The woman turned the coin over in her hand and froze. Her attentive eyes, red from the market smoke, scanned the coin. The avarice in those eyes betrayed my error. I'd given her something of great value and I thought to snatch it back, but the next thing I knew she'd thrust it at me.

"This is yours, child. Keep it." Having denied temptation, she would no longer look at me, gazing instead at the ratfin. "Have a ratfin, then. Take two. This here's a nice sibling pair."

She pointed at two: a fluffy, fat one in a corner and the thin lacy one I'd had my eye on. Given permission, I didn't hesitate. I herded them into my bell-shaped wire cage and locked the clasp. They smelled of damp fur and the mullet, eel, and loche they ate. I loved the smell of the fur and fin and took it as a comfort. That was the one failing of Mu: There were no ratfin there. As I turned away, the woman stopped me. She put a fist in my shoulder and thrust me around.

"Here then," she said, when I came round to face her. On her palm lay a second gold coin. "Take it. Take it, quick. It's yours; I know it. I don't want trouble."

Startled, I snatched it up. It's a strange thing, as a small girl, to inspire fear. I see now, it was an essential, early, life-shaping experience. I felt shame. I wanted to hide. I put the coin in my breast pocket where it thumped against its mate and hung heavy in its tight nest. I thought to ask the woman where the coin had come from and would have turned back, but then I realized I'd had two ratfin from her for no price at all. I hurried off as she shooed me before she could discover I was no threat and demand payment.

Of course, I met the woman again later. La Merde was a small, close peak. She was a friend of grandmother's and an Iron Blood, too.

That day, I wasn't in a hurry to get home. I explored down another narrow street and in the middle of it I found a stone bridge across the canal trickling down to the sea. I sat on this bridge and in its lonely crevice, surrounded by high walls coated with thick, pungent yellow moss. I peered in at the ratfin. They curled at the back of the cage. The brother, the tawny fluffy one, crouched to sniff my finger. His lacy grey sister had less fur and more fin.

I took the coins out then and, on closer examination, could not imagine how I could be so stupid as to offer the dubious treasure up as money. It was thin and rather pliable, and the gold had a green cast. The decoration on the coin was worn. Later, I made a paper tracing of the pattern. There were swirls and waves on one side. On the other, wavy lines sprawled crowned by a spiked circle. The coins had an odd feel, a bit rubbery and soft. The pictures on it looked raised, as if the images were embossed, but the surface felt smooth, but convex. The sides lifted to my fingertips and if I looked too long at them shadows appeared to flow over the surface.

At home, I found a fishhook and I thought to pierce the soft coin. When I pressed the tip of the hook into the coin, I hesitated and stopped. Instead, I wound a metal wire around the outside and affixed a chain to the end of it. I made a necklace, so the chain was visible around my neck, but the coin hung low beneath my clothing against my breastbone. I hid the other coin in my back of the closet in one of grandmother's pointy black boots. From then on, I spent a great deal of my time at the stone bridge, even at night, reading pamphlets under the streetlamp.

The pamphlets were political protests in the form of comics with thinly veiled criticisms of General Balor and calls to action: Iron Blood Jo vs. General Balfour, Iron Blood Jo Stops the Flood, and my favorite, Iron Blood Jo Returns to Sea. The printing of these materials was expensive, and it was under that pretext--for the conservation of resources--that the soldiers, once they took over the town in earnest, halted their production. Also, for our benefit, as they said, they instigated curfews. In the end, the enemy ruled us. None of this martial law kept us safe.

Once school began, I read textbooks: *The History of Pacifica Isles, Flora and Fauna of the Greater Northwest*, and what grew to be my favorite, *Maritime Knowledge and Oceans,* written by Saul Tillitat, my grandfather. They were dry books to be sure, but I lit them with my imagination.

I learned that my grandfather had been a well-respected scholar and philanthropist. My grandparents had owned the highest point on La Merde. He'd had the foresight to buy it. As the waters encroached, they had opted to give the land to the townspeople for the farms and the market. Their own house was the next highest point and then the university. The water, the ocean around me, was rising and growing more corrosive each year. The triangle of ocean I could see from the attic window grew darker purple and red. With the corrosion, grew the anger of the people crowded on pinnacles of land and General Balor stoked the fear to raise his armies and control the remaining land and its trapped people.

I, however, was always in love with water. I loved the sound of water dripping from the rooftops, streaming down the gutters, trickling through the canal, lapping under the bridge, lapping up from the ocean and soaking the streets. I loved the plop of droplets onto the cobblestones and the tap and plash of rain on the petals and leaves in grandmother's gardens. In my baths, I loved watching the steam rise and the way it moistened my skin and then flowed in rivulets from my budding breasts. I imagined building cities of stone with canals, funnels, and fountains of water. I began to sketch them and filled page after page in my notebook with pictures of drowned cities.

One day, I was exploring in one of the dusty rooms down the West wing in grandmother's mansion. In a closet I came across sheaths of sketching. At first, I thought they were my own, that someone had stolen them from my room and rummaged through them here. But the papers were older I saw, and they were not depictions of streets. They were rows and hedges--grandmother's garden and many imagined ones.

I took them downstairs and sought nana out in her warm room beside the kitchen.

"Yes, those are mine, child."

I showed her my own drawings.

"Ah, you've inherited the habit too. Come draw beside me sometimes. It gets lonely in here."

I spent more time in grandmother's room after that drawing and listening to her stories. I thought of Octavia Street, how my imagined place had had a physical location.

"Nana, is this a real place?"

"Your grandfather thought so, but he wouldn't leave me to find out."

"What happened to grandfather?"

"Well, he left me anyway. He drown. It was an accident, on the water. It was a disease of the blood."

One day, I would see that the place we imagined, Grandmother and I, was all one city. Mu was in our blood.

~ 3 ~

GRANDMOTHER'S FUNERAL

As I grew into my adolescence, I spent less time at home and more in the market. I loved to sit on the bridge with my books and sketch or read. I loved the feel of the thick mists that hung in the market--before they began to burn with acid.

The neighborhood grew more populous over the years, and it seemed that when I lowered my head into my book the streets had been empty, but when I looked up the cobblestones could scarcely be seen, they were so trodden. The streets were now filled with soldiers, a few frightened people and us--youth.

Whatever were we doing, I wonder now. Just before the war we were carrying on as if we were merely growing up and had no special role to play. I could have been frightened too; had I been paying attention.

Instead, I started spending all my time sneaking out of grandmother's house. Although I'm sure now she knew. Surely, the doors creaked. There's no one so loud as a sneak. And I went dancing at the club we all frequented.

As I began to look up more often, with rapidly growing awareness, I watched the youths dressed in black and rust heading down narrow Hector Street into some establishment. The placard over the threshold changed constantly, but the place and the crowd were always the same.

I was too young, but I got in the first time I ventured.

"You look young for your age, doll," the doorman mocked.

I was 13. In truth, I have always looked exactly my age. Even transformed as an elder, when people saw me, they could tell I had been around a while, too long, really. My purpled skin was an ageless mix of wrinkles and ocean shine, but there was a transparent, aged look to my eyes.

First, the club, our place, was called Pyrrha then Astra, then Merops, but we, the youth who went there were the same and always dressed in rust black. I was there through all the club's incantations, but I loved it best, at the end, when it was Merops.

When you came inside the club, they tied a bit of hemp around your wrist to mark you. Come to think of it, maybe grandmother noted those tattered strands about my wrist as I spooned my breakfast porridge. They tried their best to keep the place free of soldiers, but the sympathetic ones got in their rust red uniforms. We drank mugs of mulled wine and cranberry cordials. So, maybe Nana noted my bleary, dreamy, red-rimmed eyes and smelled the spice on me.

We lived at grandmother's house for several years. It would seem like no time at all in the Mulian scheme, but I do dwell on those years excessively. I remember every quiet, lonely moment of my angst-ridden youth. I still grieve for every pet.

Fluffy brother ratfin, Behn, lived a peaceful life and died a peaceful death of natural causes in his cage. I just found him still one morning, but sister ratfin, Selis, had the misfortune of managing to escape her cage. She became unpleasant in her brother's absence snarling when anyone approached the cage. I often heard her scrabbling at night and the clasp to the cage had loosened over the years. Now I suppose she might have been ill, but I thought at the time she had just become bad-tempered. One morning the cage was empty. I didn't say anything to the household, but the scent betrayed her. Selis had scuttled away into the furnace and the char man found her tiny bones.

We die like we live.

I purchased the next ratfin from the same woman, Murine, at the market. He was a smart one with a bit of a gold sheen to his black fins. He was an especially long-lived and trainable pet and Az spent most of his life wrapped around my neck--a living stole of claw, teeth, and fin. He scraped and nibbled there. My neck was often scratched and pink. Az liked to ride on my shoulders, and was a most amiable, affectionate ratfin, but he also liked to bite at clothes. The necks of my black sweaters were always frayed.

I'm sure it looked strange, but I didn't mind.

Then, around the time when I was preparing to enter university, my grandmother became truly ill. Looking back, maybe I could have remembered some odd things she said and how she started repeating the same stories of my grandfather in those days leading up to her stroke--a clot of blood in the brain. Even if I'd guessed at the trouble to come, what could I have done?

She fell in the cobblestone market but refused to let anyone carry her to the clinic. Two men brought her home lifting her between them. I knew them from Merops, I thought, and nodded.

My mother thanked them, crying.

"Ain't 'nought, she were light," they said placing her on her bed in the small room beside the kitchen, a room she rarely left after that.

I recalled how she'd said the room had been lonely when I was a child and invited me to draw with her and spent more time with her there, during her illness, I resumed drawing, but now mostly I listened to her. I see now that when I'd been a child, it was not likely she who was lonely and wanted a child to sit with her. Instead, she had seen what I was: small and in a strange place and without my familiar things. That kindness came back to her--as kindnesses will. Kindnesses nibble below the surface of events like hungry little fishes after the lichens under floating lotus leaves.

So, grandmother's kindness resurfaced to help her in her illness. I sat with her and listened.

She repeated the story of grandfather over and over again. Her brain lapped at that memory like waves in a bay. It wasn't until later when I dove under the water and entered the sea cave that I understood the significance of what she had been saying. In Mu, I understood, my grandfather had gone underwater before me.

I also took up my drawings again, and I was more skilled now with my lines and arches, perspectives, and scale. My sketches were better, but what struck me was how they were the same as the drawings of my youth. Every time I drew the imaginary city, Octavia, thinking I would undertake a completely different design, it came out the same. I knew the layout of the city and where everything should go. I knew where the large meeting dome went and the stadium and the large open lawn and grandmother's gardens and the storeroom. It did not feel right to draw it in any other way.

One day, Nana was telling her story again and she seemed far away, her eyes shimmery with tears. I did not know if I even existed for her still. Then, she turned to me.

"Nata," she said, she had not used my name in a while. "Don't you leave him. When you love, you stay."

Her voice was stern and I remembered it from her arguments with mother, the ones that coincided with father's rare letters, when, I know, her advice had been exactly the opposite.

She didn't ask me to promise. In fact, she said plainly, "Be careful, child. Be careful with promises, especially to a dying old woman and an ancestor," she said. "Though it pleases me."

But I did want to please her, I said, "I will. I'll stay."

It seemed to relax her.

Grandmother's funeral was held in the blue-domed stone Iron Blood Church. Her body was displayed on the altar during the service.

When we filed by, we showed deference to the waxen figure. This was Nana, her soul lingered nearby, until it was carried out on the waves to go in search of its next incarnation.

We said, our usual refrains, "Praise the Mountaintop." Yet, I wondered, why we worshipped that which was receding and distant instead of the life rising around us? Why not say, "Praise Water"?

It's cruel, but the person who must grieve the most, must plan the funeral. My mother, who so sunk by grief was barely capable of standing, made grandmother's arrangements. The church smelled of rose lotion. All of Nana's friends must have slathered it on for the occasion. An iron-rose tang emanated from the perspiring congregation. The air was moist, hot, and acidic. My inhalations burned.

Pastor Rotwasser's voice was a reassuring drone interrupted occasionally by sniffles, catches of breath, muffled coughs, and the raspy unfurling of handkerchiefs.

Rotwasser had evidently not been a close friend of Nana's. He did not know her or us. To him, grandmother was only the land she and grandfather had given and her death an opportunity to remind the other elders in the audience of their coming doom. He was clearly a man who feared death. All he knew how to do was proselytize to the living, and worse, he brought in politics.

We all felt the presence of soldiers nodding in approval at the back of the church. Clearly, they'd made their presence felt here in the past. The church was no safe haven, no high ground. I wondered whether the soldiers had gathered in the back of the church in their blue uniforms to pay their respects. My grandmother was beloved in town, and more so for being grandfather's life mate.

There was really nothing funny about it, but the contrast between Rotwasser's somber tone and his glib words made me want to laugh.

"It is better to bleed into the ocean at your sea-fairing than to jostle the oceans of your body into waves at the market," said Rotwasser. "For we are all going into the sea, and we must allow the waves to rise to us sooner than later. The salt of blood is better than the salt of the earth or even the salt of the sea. We raise it to our lips and drink a toast. A wise man knows his blood belongs to the ocean, while a poor man spills his blood on the shore."

It might have been a thoughtful parable to contemplate, but not at a funeral! I would have said, "The ocean surrounds me and provides me peace because I float in it. I'm lifted by the waves and the warmth of my blood and the salt. Because I bleed on the shore, I know I shall bleed well into the sea." It was the same sentiment, but a gentler expression.

Suddenly, with grandmother's death, I grew up. I became an adult. I looked at the pastor, at my broken mother, at the soldiers smirking in the doorway of the church--all these figures of authority and I saw that they were fallible and, in many ways, extremely unorganized. I looked at grandmother's friends who were feeble in all aspects, but their stalwart faces and I imagined I saw them nod. I saw among them Murine, the ratfin seller, and she did nod I am certain. Just in recognition, perhaps, but I took it as affirmation. It was my time to seize the future.

"It is better to bleed," Rotwasser repeated, and then I sputtered.

My body shook. I put my hand to my mouth, but I grinned beyond the shield of it. Undercover, I chuckled, and that sound released the floodgates. I began to giggle.

At first no one looked, but then I saw the eyes of the gray-haired ladies dart at me. Az ran around the back of my neck. Mother had been too distraught to forbid me taking him to the funeral. I'd hid him under my black felt collar where he chewed threads. I attempted to restrain my laughter with thoughts of dead Ratfin: Ea's drowned body and Selis' charred bones.

We die like we live.

To this day, I have a tendency toward spontaneous amusement in inappropriate places. I can often contain it by casting my eyes downward and imagining dead ratfin. Too much somberness or certainty strikes me as absurd. My grandmother gave me this perspective. Thinking about those small limp bodies still and black mollifies me. A ratfin's a tiny creature, but all death looms large and carries sunken, sobering weight.

At grandmother's funeral, I had not yet learned this trick, however. I began to think about my grandmother, and how I'd brought her a piece of watercress cake from her favorite market vendor. In her last days, grandmother hadn't had much of an appetite. I'd thought I'd bring her something more enticing than the tepid bowls of rice she'd been spooning down.

It hadn't been one of her good days, at first, when I brought her the slice of cake. She had forgotten me that day.

"You're bringing me poison, soldier. No, take it away," she said.

I brought the cake close to her, but she cringed and looked ready to cry. I prepared to leave it. Then, she must have smelled the frosting. Her expression changed. She looked at the slice of cake as if examining its molecular structure. These moments of lucidity were better than those in which she merely remembered my name. She looked at the world as if she had returned from inside herself with secret knowledge. She scrutinized her surroundings. I'd come with a fork and handed it to her now.

She'd detached a corner of cake holding it daintily with only a faint tremor of her hand. The frosting and cake crumbs disappeared in her mouth. She savored it. Clearly, she had never enjoyed a bite of cake this thoroughly. She looked perfectly content for a moment, just enough time for me to feel satisfaction and pride at my gift.

Then, she'd wretched. She'd spewed a trail of white down the front of her blouse and dribbled onto the cake like a macabre topping. It smelled acidic.

I was horrified, but grandmother gave out a choking laugh.

"Stand down, soldier."

I'd started to laugh at the absurdity and the hopelessness. Grandmother had not even the enjoyment of this cake left to her, and it seemed right. How could she enjoy it when she did not even know her own name? I wiped the spittle off her lips and blouse and that's when she returned in a rare moment.

She looked down. "Oh, my favorite cake. See child, I'm done for."

Then she proceeded to tell me in great, startling detail of the first time she'd ever had the cake. She remembered ridiculous information about that moment: the precise shape of the cake, the thickness of the frosting, and the exact cost of it down to the penny. She remembered the people in the market on the day she bought the cake.

"I was on a date with your grandfather. He was like your father in more ways than one. He was a fabulous swimmer," she looked sad. "Promise me, you'll set me out to sea when I'm done here."

I grew somber.

"Nana, all Iron Bloods have a proper sea-fairing."

"That's right. So...?"

I hesitated. Always be careful with promises, Nana had taught me that. It was like a test. The way she emphasized, "Promise."

"You promise, then?"

"Yes, I'll see after your sea-fairing."

She sighed. "Thank you, Nata."

She pronounced my name slowly and certainly in a mocking tone as if, of course, she knew it always. "Now, thanks to you, my last memory will be of barfing up my favorite food."

We both laughed so hard, grandmother making rasping, wheezy cackles.

My mother checked in on us. "Is everything all right?"

When had laughter become cause for concern?

"Oh yes, it's all right. It's all right. We're just dying of laughter," Nana said.

Her hacking gasps of laughter did sound like choking.

As I like to remember it, she died peacefully late that night.

I couldn't think about dying ratfin in the church at grandmother's funeral. I could only think of Nana puking all over her favorite cake and I could not stop laughing. Finally, everyone was staring at me and even the pastor stopped talking. He glared down at me as if I were a berserker laughing during battle. My mother put her hand on my arm, eventually.

I was laughing so hard I was crying. Mollified, I could not stop. I felt horrible. What if people thought my laughter meant I did not care for her? That almost sobered me, but I immediately heard grandmother saying, "I'm done for," in a childish voice. All propriety was gone. It was absurd. It was sacrilege. I could see that cake so clearly, its decadence and desirability meaningless. Sugar, a substance useless against water and death.

My mother hauled me out of the church. She pulled me down the aisle. Her fingernails poked through the skin of my forearm, but I didn't stop laughing, even in front of all those glaring faces half-shielded by black handkerchiefs, until we were out in the vestibule. Then I was silent, awaiting my mother's fury. Although she had never struck me, I expected to be slapped. Instead, mother pulled me down on the bench and slumped over me with sobs of relief.

"I'm so glad to be out of there for a moment," she said. "It's the hardest thing I've ever done. Harder even than leaving your father."

We hugged each other. I regained my equilibrium. My laughter turned to tears. Then when we turned back to enter the church there was Pastor Rotwasser behind us and a soldier decorated with badges.

"This gentleman would like to speak with you, Bettany," Rotwasser said.

The soldier took mother's arm and pulled her close. I stayed close though, so I could just hear.

"We want her blood," he said.

They would siphon the iron blood from Nana's body before they would let us take her from the church.

Mother stopped: arrested and confused. After the service, my grandmother's body was supposed to be taken to the sea in a procession. She had asked to be lowered off the dock into the rust-stained water.

So, this was the purpose of the soldiers gathered in the back of the church. They wore their blue uniforms, looked on, and waited until they could complete their duty--to drain grandmother's corpse of blood.

Had the pastor been better at his job, we would never have known. He would have just let them take her body to the back and take her blood. Likely, we wouldn't have noticed her desiccation before she was set into the water. Grandmother had become so thin, as she walked beside death. Then the water would have quickly eroded her.

This pastor, however, brought the men before my mother--as though to ask permission. There was never a question about that though. General Balor's soldiers had assumed authority long before they'd officially claimed it.

"I thought you would want to know," Pastor Rotwasser said.

"It will just take a moment," said the sergeant.

"I'm sorry for your loss," said one of the younger men. I recognized him from Merops. I'd seen him out of the uniform that marked him as one of Balor's men in a rust version that made him one of ours. Surely, he was my enemy now, but I loved him anyway as one of my youths.

The sergeant kept mother engaged. I didn't hear the whole conversation, but I heard my mother screaming. Everyone at the funeral did. Then they heard the soldiers yelling back.

In the chapel, they grabbed at the body. The old men threw up their arms and the soldiers locked their meaty hands around their elders' feeble wrists.

"Shame. Shame," the old women chanted in horror, Murine, Hattie, my Aunt Virgie and Cousin Tolly among them. They were shocked. They didn't know what to do or say. That generation was only then used to thinking of the rising, rust sea as the enemy, not each other. They hadn't yet transferred their hatred and fear to the blue uniforms.

In the end, the soldiers achieved their purpose. They took grandmother's body and drained her.

I would have fought them. I remembered my promise to Nana--a proper sea-fairing.

But my mother saved me, "Leave. Go. I won't have you here for this. It won't change anything. Go!"

She chased me away. She saved me from trouble that time, but my time was coming. The waters were rising and there was little land left to us. No one would be safe in the days ahead, especially not those of Iron Blood.

I walked up Octavia Street alone to the house, Tillitat Manor, at the top of the hill. It was springtime now and the pink and white flowers my grandmother had pressed into her lotions were in bloom as were the fruit trees in the yard. The place should have been occupied by a few of my grandmother's old friends awaiting the reception. Funerals must always be followed by food. Instead, the people who loved Nana were at the church losing a battle with soldiers gaining bruises on their thin, fragile skins.

There was a warm salad and that was fine. I went into the sunlit orangerie and filled a bowl with ripe fruits. One of my mother's friends came--Reese, a man vying to be her lover. I had scrutinized him for signs of my father, but he was shy around her and did not give her gifts, which made him seem wanting, but also harmless.

"They've taken Bettany, your mother, to jail," he said. "Virgie and Tolly, too. I'm trying to get them out. It will be all right. But can you take care of yourself tonight?"

What choice did I have? I have often found myself alone in times of trouble.

~ 4 ~

MEROPS

Left alone in the big house, I went up to my room where I felt inside the dark half of my closet. I could only distinguish among the black clothes by touch: the twill jumper, the velvet pants, the silk shirt, and the lace blouse. I meant to put on my grandmother's black clothes and go out. I took off the black mourning dress and wore just the slip with a black petticoat underneath to give it flounce. I dabbed black around my eyes and red on my lips. I added black and rust striped stockings. I took the strange coin out from toe and wore my grandmother's pointed shoes. I tied the rust red kerchief around my neck.

I went to Merops. That night I met him. Fresh from my grandmother's funeral, dressed for winter in the heart of spring, I took my sketchbook to the club to dream of waterlogged cities. I met my soul mate there in the strangest of circumstances. I met my twin soul, too.

It became important to understand the difference.

A soul mate attracts in an overwhelming way with an overwhelming passion. A twin soul applies a more subtle presence. A soul mate arrives as a tsunami crashing over the land and a twin soul is the ocean washing persistently over the shore. A wise person understands the difference and knows who is in their heart.

Separation from a soul mate causes a painful rending with doubt and desperation whereas physical separation from a twin soul can be endured. It is a soft sorrow. Real separation from a twin soul is not possible. The souls stride in unison.

I met my souls on the evening of grandmother's aborted seafairing.

The next day my relatives would be released from jail (Reese, my mother's boyfriend was a lawyer--he dealt with land rights not criminal law--but what he knew was enough) and the processional was held. My grandmother's desiccated corpse, drained of her Iron Blood, was hoisted above the street by her dedicated Iron Blood friends and carried down to the Rust Sea.

My grandmother died at age 91 as had her mother and grandmother before her. My mother expected to die at age 91 also.

And I? I never expected I would live that long. Everything was on the brink in my lifetime. The corrosive waters were rising. War was overtaking every last island. The timeline of history was pronounced, and it had a palpable ridge like a raised scar. My father had been right to hide our Iron Blood. The soldiers first drained the blood from corpses for their experiments. Then, after they had some success, they wanted to drain us alive.

When they lowered grandmother's body into the sea, the waves began to churn as though dancing to the sound of the pipes played by her friends. My mother clutched Reese and wept. The soldiers were absent. They were somewhere standing ghoulishly over a vat of grandmother's cold blood, I imagined.

However, I do not want to remember that morning and what followed too quickly. I want to tell of what happened the night before when I was observing death in all my actions and embracing the darkness of music and dance. My memory clings to this origin point like kelp to a pebbled shore. I can feel every second of it like tiny stones aginst my skin.

I loved the club best when it was Merops, by then I knew the music and I recognized everyone--but not too well. The club always had a dreamy quality.

My hazed memory of Merops was colored by wine. In Mu, there was no wine. Instead, we would recreate the drunken experience by remembering Merops.

I passed the cobbled bridge and entered under the red and black "Merops" placard. Music vibrated out into the street. The alleyway smelled of cloves. I descended into the dark, toward the drums, and approached the candlelit bar. The club had always been a refuge for me, but until then I had thought of it only in terms of amusement. I hadn't made the connection yet between the growing number of soldiers on the street and the growing number of youths in the club. I knew that we were all Iron Bloods. We wore the deep rich rust color and flaunted it here, as we would not do on the street.

As a young woman, I could be excruciatingly languid in my movements, like a slow river, but Deuc was more languid still. He was singing on stage when I first laid eyes on him. His dark eyes shone in his pale face. He moved slowly and waved his hands in gestures I found unbearably attractive. From the very first time I noticed his movement; he rippled out from my heart like he belonged there. I loved his slender, ethereal quality. He moved as though his body were an apparition. He did not look like a threat of any kind. It would surprise me later--every time--how strong he was when he restrained me.

Twice, he saved my life by the strength of his own hands. Once he saved me when it is certain I would have met my everlasting death and when I no longer assumed I would live another day.

Now, to state clearly, this was exactly what happened the first time I met Deuc. I walked in the stone entryway, approached the bar, and asked for wine.

"Mulled's the special tonight. Perfect on a damp night. Have it, then?" the bartender asked.

Az, my dear ratfin, peeked over my shoulder as I assented, "Mellow."

At least this was how I imagined the conversation went. If I could go back in time, I would pay closer attention. I would try to see the waves riding into place. That's my specialty, after all.

This I know: A steam of hot cloves rose off the mulled wine as I grasped the scrolled handle of the thick mug. Though, it's true, my memory of this may not be from that particular night. A collection of nights followed thereafter when mulled wine became my drink of choice at Merops.

Now, this was important: That the bartender handed me a mug and I walked away without looking back. When I felt too confident in my perceptions, I would remember this moment. I walked away and sat in my usual corner--my usual corner!--that's how often I'd come to the bar and then walked away, heedless, beside the stage. It was no different than many other nights until Deuc came on stage.

I had never--swear fealty!—never, feared death more than the moment I saw Deuc. My heart seized. I was drained crisp, sponge dry. My lungs hurt. I clenched the mug and sucked the lip to steady myself. The steam had a sting to it and the wine sourness. When I saw Deuc, I began a romance with death. He became that to me.

I have since gained perspective and even from a weathered distance of time and war, I know that its true that the moment I saw Deuc everything changed. My feelings were true then, though not as true as they would be later. My feelings were real, that night, I was even right about the wine. It was sour under the spices and too dry, hence the special on mulled wine. In Deuc's radiance, I grew more discerning. On subsequent nights the wine would be sweeter, but never headier.

I turned toward the stage, drink in hand, and began, as we all did, to fall in love with Deuc. He stood on the stage and played the lute. He vibrated and peered out at us, his vibrations, with liquid black eyes. When I danced, I thought he stared at me, but everyone thought that.

He sang too, but I couldn't make out the words and didn't care. I danced, rocking my blossoming hips and the dark, wet lust I carried between those bones. I found the community of rust red dancers mesmerizing. In that time, everything was sinking and there seemed to be no escape from the aquatic life that chased us. The older people clung to the tops of their islands. I was of the new people: the generation that began to welcome the water. We were practicing there in Merops. I watched us dancing like waves.

Merops was a magical gathering place--a magnificent backdrop for Deuc. When I took a seat at a table and he took a break, he came and sat beside me, and we talked over steaming wine. I don't remember what we talked about. Whatever, I was rapt. I imagined he was equally captivated, but I did not yet understand how Deuc's consciousness was ruled by music, a strong current that could become an undertow. I was swept away by him headed far out past the barriers of my beliefs. That should have been a lighthouse signal, but I didn't understand the warning. Of my own free will, I would certainly crash.

When he returned to the stage, I would stand as close to him as I could from below and will him to look down at me. When he sang "Lava Hex," "Volcanoes undertow the scoria rises. Heed the river. Heed the ocean. Watch the heat." He would walk to the edge of the stage and lean back with his legs wide. The club would chant, "Heed the river. Heed the ocean." There was energy between us that I wanted to amplify. He would make eye contact with me, and I would imagine that this song was written for me. I didn't notice he looked at others too. Too preoccupied with the cays of my own griefs, I didn't understand his oceanic lyrics until later.

I went back to his room above the club many times in a besotted state. Every time, we just talked or even stared at each other. We lay on the bed. Sometimes he'd take my hand and stroke it. I wanted him to kiss me, but he wouldn't. I didn't know what he was waiting for. He made it clear he slept with everyone. I was not to fall in love with him, but it was too late. I was already in love. I fell in love with him instantly.

"It improves my music. I want to connect with everyone," he said. It was his philosophy, that we were all connected. It was a particularly painful point of view for a young lovestruck woman. I wanted him all to myself.

For months, I feared I would not see Deuc again. At times I felt I'd imagined him in a dream of clove-laden steam and had only the hemp rope of Merops on my wrist to remind me. I thought everyone must know him, had seen him in the same way I saw him. Deuc so fascinated my mind that I dwelled over him at every moment. To this day, I can hardly explain what came over me. He was standing on stage. He was singing. He was swaying side to side, and he was smoldering at me, at the crowd. He looked piercing. I was jealous of everyone, thinking they knew him and knew how to find him. I was right to be. Most people did know Deuc and had been to his room upstairs above Merops.

That night I fell in love and the next morning buried my grandmother. I'm ashamed to say that while I watched my grandmother's husk corrode into the Rust Sea, as I watched it devour her, I thought of Deuc and how I wanted his wet kisses.

~ 5 ~

UNIVERSITY

After grandmother's death I enrolled in university. I spent my days there and many nights in Merops. The soldiers' presence was becoming more obvious in town. They were numerous and they often harassed Iron Blood students. There were blood checks and stops. They pricked our skins and recorded the level of "rust" therein. Students walked around with fresh wounds upon their shoulders where once we carried only books.

Merops was our haven.

At university, I began studying marine biology and was approached by professor Alexandria Belo. She sought me out. She knew I was of Iron Blood.

"I knew your grandfather," she said. "I want you to work on my new Seasteading project."

Using grandfather's technology and her theories on marine life, she wanted to build oceanic platforms that could resist the rust sea. The earth's islands were sinking, we would build our own.

I became engrossed in Seasteading and found my calling. I was going to build the place I'd always dreamed of. Later, I realized that Belo's research (and before her time, my grandfather's) was what had tipped the soldiers off and caused trouble for us Iron Bloods, but I could not blame her. Someone had to try to make a new way.

Around this same time, I became disenchanted with Deuc. At Merops, he was everyone's center, but even at the time this delusion angered me. It was ludicrous. We are all our own center.

I imagined them all grasping, gasping, and cascading after him. Every night, I drank my wine, looked for Deuc, and became more furious over my enchantment: the spell I was under, which was not, as it turned out, all his doing.

On this night, I found the music too loud, and I wrapped a scarf around my ears. It muffled Deuc's voice as though he was singing underwater. The drums and the keyboard remained just as loud and I could make out his words, but I was at a distance. I listened to the song.

The people rise up while the waters are rising,
They live on pinnacles of land;
The Riptides strip the land of trees,
They take to the waters to live.
Land so little, so much water,
Madrona, oak, pine raft on the water,
Land so little, so much water,
Madrona, oak, pine raft on the water,
The people fear the waters rising,
Living on pillars of land;
The Riptides float on the waters rising,
Just obey their commands.
The ship Kyklopes and the captains, too,
All float over the rising Rust Sea,
The Rust Sea binds, the Rust Sea binds,
Us all together, close. Us all together, close.

The song was romanticizing the Riptiders, who most people saw as selfish pirates who had stolen every islands' remaining wood which was more resistant to the corrosion than metal. Later, Deuc would explain to me his reasoning, his fascination with the pirates, but now I couldn't hear it. I felt rejected. The lyrics seemed like premonitions. I needed to get out. I needed to go away. I told myself I was done being in Deuc's thrall. I retreated to a dark place in the back of the club, one of Merops' many dark corners, to sip my wine. I was watching a different man dancing. I'd never seen anyone twist and spiral like this. He dropped to the floor and came up in a spin like a porpoise. He seemed completely in the throes of the drums, and I understood this. I enjoyed watching the experience and seeing how it looked. I had felt what he was feeling. It was like seeing inside myself. He seemed oblivious to everything but the music and the dance, but after the set he walked straight up to me in a steady line approaching my sphere of darkness. He put a coin down on the table and pushed it across to me. I was startled, but briefly pretended not to recognize it.

Finally, drunk, I said, "Another one?". “Why are people always giving these to me?” I muttered.

He picked it up and inspected it.

"But isn't this yours? It fell out on the dance floor."

It was then that I noticed the chain, the dulled silver links.

"Oh, yes," I said and snatched it up and refastened it around my neck, which took several tries. He did not offer to help.

"Who gives these to you?"

I looked into his green eyes and found myself talking. I told him about the pawnshop and about Murine, the street vendor who sold me my ratfin. He sat beside me and listened. I told him about my violent father and my escape to La Merde. I told him about Ea, the dead ratfin I had dropped overboard. These coins contained my most precious stories. I was filled with a rising tide of mulled wine and my throat opened up and my stories spilled out.

His name was Georgios. He was the bartender at Merops. I'd seen him many times, he'd given me my mugs of mulled wine, but I never really saw him until that night when he was dancing.

After I paused in my talk, he reached forward and lifted the coin off my chest. He inspected it a long time and rubbed a finger over the surface as if he were imprinting its picture into his skin. It felt like he was looking into my heart.

"Will you be here next weekend?"

"Of course."

But I wasn't. None of us were. The soldiers came to Merops that night. They darkened the doors with their blue uniforms. They made the music stop. They shut our meeting place down.

In my memory, I dwell on Merops. Someday I imagine I will swim to sunken La Merde and dive deep to find the underwater ruins of that place that I loved. Although it was the people that made it special, and they are everywhere and nowhere.

At that time, I was so obsessed with seasteading I hardly noticed the absence of Merops. Some will say this was a mistake--to let anything go without a fight, but then the fighting never seemed to advance our cause. We had nowhere to go and nothing to ask for. I poured over the blueprints, and my studies exhausted me. Looking back, I hardly understand how I could have been so tired with a perfect, painless body. I was depleted. Now I have verve for everything, the life of the sea within my soul, but, physically, I ache.

Working on the seastead project, I met Timbol, another of Professor Belo's recruits. He and I took out the rusty boats. We sloshed through the water in our bioproof-slickers, waders, and shoulder-length gloves. They offered scant protection and would corrode in a day's time. We dug into the sand beds up to our elbows.

"Hey Timbol," I vamped. "Striptease."

We laughed about the protective outfits and mocked each other's appearance, but both of us had burns on our upper arms and thighs where we'd been careless and let the tainted water splash. As the summer wore on, our faces were patchy with red from the rust ocean air. The iron was strong in our nostrils. It amazes me, looking back, that we could have been so absorbed in academics while there was a war going on. When the people you love are dying it becomes impossible for most people to think of the future, but even while the war snuffed lives, Timbol and I--and the rest of the Seasteaders--planned. We dreamt of another life, another way. It was a power that pulsed within us. It was not only our youth, although it was that, too.

Beneath the water, the older prehistoric creatures had somehow adapted to the rust water, while the younger fish died off. There were big oily barnacles with thick blackish red shells. In the water, occasionally coming close to shore when they were ill, were shark, squid, and whales. They were large hungry creatures with little to feed upon. We speculated that somewhere in the ocean there were fresh springs with more food for these creatures, or how else could they live? There was a gap in our knowledge of this new sea that kept us at a distance.

"So, Alex really thinks this is our salvation?" Timbol said looking at water where we were surveying the shore slathered in red algae. We called our professor Alex now. We had been to her house. We had met her lover, Neena, an English professor. They had served us wine and brined vegetables.

"Well, it's not like we have much choice. The land's going under," I said.

"There's Hiryana, Cos, Faroe, Corvo..." he named off some of the remaining islands. "There's still high ground and places like Noronha where the water will probably never reach."

Timbol and I repeated this argument over the value of our work often. We were reassuring ourselves. Timbol liked to spout the Peaker philosophy--that there was always higher ground out there somewhere. Some dreamed of a mythical mountain--Rainier--that rose into the sky high above where the water could ever reach.

"Praise the mountaintop. Praise top!" he'd bend his head back and point his finger into the sky. He was mocking them, but either of us would have been grateful to find the Peaker's paradise on Rainier.

"There's war, but this is our land," Timbol became serious. "Just because we can't see it, why would we abandon it? We know it's here. I know every hill and dip and shoreline and peak."

"You do, but years from now. No one else will. The time you grew up here will just be stories. They won't think of anything, but the killing sea. It's not habitable."

"They," Timbol said. "Whoever is left. We'll need a map, a cartographer, so they'll remember what's below."

"Sure," I said. "Sure." Not really caring what lay below at that time. We would leave it behind I thought.

The Seasteaders had a plan for the personnel who would be needed on the seastead: a cook, an agriculturalist, a welder, a marine biologist (Timbol claimed that role), and Timbol's cartographer. Professor Belo was working on recruiting. Of course, Professor Belo, Neena, Timbol and I would be aboard. It was a good plan, but we didn't know that Neena had no desire to go aboard and no skills that would be of use on the stead. We certainly didn't imagine that Professor Belo would be dead by the time we launched.

"You plan for everything," Timbol said to me one day cutting off our regular argument. "I'd follow you anywhere. I don't know why I bother to argue."

I didn't deny his submission. I was getting used to the idea: People followed me. They trusted me.

"I like it when you ask questions though. It makes me think harder about the answers." I said. "To meet uncertainty, you have to be organized," I muttered to myself. It was becoming my mantra. I underestimated the level of organization required though. I thought it could just be a few others, a small island, and me.

Many people avoided the water. Most older folks (Alexandria Belo was a notable exception) clung to the land. Professor Belo's project was twofold. First, she would discover the secret formula to our Iron Blood that would enable us to counteract the corrosiveness of the sea. This was the work my grandfather had begun. Then, she had planned to build platforms on the water where we would live.

"There's one more thing," she said. "When we can get to it. Our objective will be to join the sea to leave the land behind. There's no need to talk of that yet. I just want you to know that's where I'm going."

On these new platforms, new societies could be built. Seasteads were raised platforms of metal with supports sunk into the sea, weighted and bound with floats. Many stragglers had erected them back in the day and they had once cluttered the sea. Then the waters had become corrosive, and the platforms rusted and sank. It was the time of the Ocean Settlers followed by the Rust Sea. None of the sea settlements had been very organized. They'd mostly been built by individuals--people's own houses. A few cities had planned centers and even a floating market existed at some point. When the seas had begun rising faster and people realized that the time for long-range planning was well past, organized thinking broke down, in as much as it had ever existed. First, came the mercenaries. Then, came the soldiers. War overflowed. It was easier for men to be awash, brainless, and compliant, than to think. There were many followers.

The La Merde University Seastead Project was funded by Marshall Camden, a wealthy trader who had lost his livelihood in the war but not his resources. Camden now gave freely to the university hoping to find a way to restore his business. When Professor Belo was too busy for me, I relied on Marshall, our benefactor. I often met with him in his house beside the ferry dock.

It was a stupid place to live. He had had to move his family up to the second story as the water rose, but he liked to be near his trading post. He also wanted to be ready to leave, to get to high ground, if the seastead didn't work out. The drive to tell him things was strong. He listened with intensity. In person, it felt like a magnetic pull, pulling your words, thoughts, and even a part of your soul out along with whatever news you had to share. I told him every detail of our work, but he kept a huge secret from me.

"Hurry the project along," he urged, at the end of every meeting. “The waters are rising.”

But I could not feel his angst. This was such an obvious statement; the way things had been all my life.

Marshall's involvement with the Seastead was his own private rebellion. A man with his wealth and power gives the illusion of freedom, but he was tied to his business. All of his time and energy went into it. All his actions were married to it. Even friendships had become investments in maintaining revenue growth. Professor Belo must have known about the more unsavory aspects of Marshall's business and his ties with General Balor.

Left alone, for a while, the university made progress. They had developed some new materials and new designs. The university was working with La Merde to begin building out onto the water. With the land sinking from beneath us, many had looked for ways to build out onto the sea, cover the waters with steel as we had once paved the earth with concrete. There were limitations to that with the corrosive salt of our sea. Professor Belo was the first person to imagine the concept in this way: That we, freed from the land, would make our own society. This idea inspired me. I imagined it was my own. Looking back, I could see how every childhood fantasy had led me to this calling.

When Belo had identified a group of Seasteaders, she invited us to meet at a party at her place by the bay.

Professor Belo and Neena had a small hut with a thatched roof by the bay. It was one room with a kitchen, with their bed covered with a red blanket and many books and a writing station. Neena brought the food to us at a long table in the brush. We sat on cushions.

Their simple home so near the water reminded me that my grandmother's home on the hill, Tillitat Manor, was luxurious. It still had wooden banisters, a Riptider's treasure.

"Now this is our team. You've likely seen each other around or in class, but this is the first time you have met as Seasteaders," she said. It was the first time she had used the word to identify us, and I marked it. "Let's go around and have introductions."

"It's a small group," I said noting just two others at the table besides Neena, Belo, Timbol and myself.

"The twins are late, but they'll be here," she said. She looked a little concerned. "I might as well make it clear before they get here. The twins are Marshall's sons. Our benefactor doesn't want to go out with us, but he wants both of his sons involved. They'll bring skills as well, I'm sure."

Timbol sat beside me.

A girl with long, straight dark hair began the introductions, "I'm Desiree. I cook and I grow my own foods. My specialty is hydroponics and spices." She did not have an easy smile. Her hair hung straight down upon her back unmoving. There was a gracefulness to her slow movements down to the way she held her fork and passed the wooden bowls.

Merl introduced himself next. He was a gruff wiry man. "I'm studying engineering and solar power. I'm going to provide the light," he said. "We've been working on water pumps and sanitation. Waste not, want not."

Timbol explained his specialty in marine biology and agriculture. He nodded at Desiree. "I'll help with the food."

"There won't be much room in our kitchen, but I'll squeeze aside."

"I meant with the growing, but, sure, I can cook, too."

Then it was my turn. Suddenly, I wasn't sure what my role was. "Oceanography, like Timbol and, well, planning."

We heard shouting from the brush and crashing footsteps.

"I'm saying don't trust them," a low voice said.

"Ha," said the other, and the voice in that one short syllable was so familiar.

The "twins" appeared. They were tall, lean, and dark-haired. I knew them immediately from Merops. I hadn't known they were Marshall's sons, and I hadn't known they were brothers. They always kept apart: Deuc on the stage and Georgios behind the bar. I felt foolish not to have seen the resemblance.

They'd clearly been arguing, and they carried in from the woods with them a dark energy. Deuc always wore a bit of a dire furrow on his face, but the intensity changed Georgios' open face completely. His eyes drooped. His broad lips compressed. Still, they greeted Belo and Neena pleasantly and sat down beside each other. They sat across from me and I gazed at them. It was the first time I'd ever seen them side by side. Now it was obvious that they were brothers, possibly even fraternal twins. They'd never looked similar before. It was disconcerting. What else had I been missing by my inattention?

"Well, you've missed the introductions." Belo said.

"No worries, we're acquainted," Deuc said. "That's the tinker. That's the pretty cook. That's the whale-lover. And that's the dreamer--who thinks she's our leader."

He pointed in turn to Merl, Desiree, Timbol, and me.

"Whiskey, whiskey, ale, and mulled wine," Georgios said, he knew us by our drink orders and I'm sure had observed our other preferences as well in Merops.

"Well, why don't you introduce yourselves and say what you will you bring to the seastead," Belo said.

"We all know Georgios makes a mean drink," Deuc said.

"And I draw, too," Georgios said shyly.

Timbol leaned over to me and whispered, "We're not the only ones thought of it, I bet that's our cartographer."

Then we tucked into the food and drink and soon the tension dissipated. We ate well. We passed the bowls round and round. Our cups were always full. Desiree ate the whole time. She was at table nibbling little bites off of every dish.

"Pass me that one," she said. "And that one."

She savored the spices.

Merl liked the mashed root vegetables best. He dug into them, poured on the truffle gravy, and ate intently at the beginning of the meal. Later, when he was sated, he regaled the rest of us with stories while we caught up and filled our bellies.

Timbol took an even portion from the dishes that were nearest him and ate and talked in equal measure.

My plate was carefully engineered, a dab of each dish. I waited to begin to eat until I had everything arranged on the plate. I took a bite here and there and saved my favorite, water chestnut stew, for last.

Desiree and Merl bonded over their love of whiskey and began to scheme for how they could distill on the seastead.

I began to feel drunk. I loved all the Seasteaders already. I was making eyes at Georgios and Deuc and imagining what it would be like to have both of them kissing me. I would remember this shamefully, blushing the next day.

At the end of the meal, Deuc took his lute out of the case. "Let me remind you why I am here."

He began to play, and his voice was beautiful. We would need him on the sea when we tired of the sound of waves.

Then, Alex stood up and made her announcement. "I'm almost there with the formula. I tried an early version on the water, and it stopped the rust. But it's been hard to get enough to work with for all the tests and variations."

I noticed then how drawn Neena looked. She was an Iron Blood, too. Alex had been draining her for her experiments.

"I need more samples and I'm hoping you will all donate," she said.

She took us aside one by one, and we went into the house. There was a damp chill to the air. It was growing dark and cold. She drew pints of blood from us all. I remembered my grandmother's body drained of blood.

There were more nights like this. In my memory, these nights seemed infinite. We danced in the woods. Deuc sang. Belo took our blood. This was our Merops under the stars. While we partied and donated, the fervor for higher ground intensified.

The army demanded that Chancellor Freelan turn over the university land for its use. He refused and was killed. We students fought back. We didn't want our university to be used for war mongering, but we lost.

I remember screaming alongside the other students in the courtyard before the archway, "No blood for war!" I was giving up my blood, but I thought my cause peaceful.

We pelted the soldiers with oranges and precious books. We threw them down as though the symbolism alone of them being hit by tomes might make an impression. It was wasteful, but with the university overrun by soldiers there would be no higher ground to store those books. It made no difference. The books would become wet and rot and corrode in the sea like everything else left behind. Balor's army shut the university down. They chased the students out or recruited them to their ranks. Our school grounds became barracks.

I offered the Seasteaders Tillitat Manor as shelter. It was on high ground and there was plenty of room. I remember the way Deuc ogled the banisters, the hungry look in his eye I wished he'd had for me.

Then, news came of Professor Belo's death.

I remember the last lecture Alexandria Belo gave. She stood in my living room, grandmother's living room. Her dark brown hair was plaited. She wore wide skirts with pockets. She was explaining the structure of the molecules she had discovered in our Iron Blood that float over the toxic water and encase the metal in a protective shell. It was this structure that would allow us to build the platforms on the water.

She talked to us about the practical applications, many of which had yet to be discovered. To me, the real mystery was where this molecule had come from. Why had it never been seen before? Belo who was known to deliver every line and every lecture with absolute certainty, sounded uncertain about this point. It was clearly a puzzle to her how it could have arrived at such a providential time and been created to suit our need. I remember that uncertainty and I also remember how solitary and strong she looked standing before us in my grandmother's living room. Belo gave imposing, urgent lectures there. Maybe the fact that we were sunk into my grandmother's old cushions added to her stature. We felt we could not learn fast enough. The Seasteaders and a few professors and students had relocated to my grandmother's house. I offered it up for classes. I knew my grandfather would have approved. The waters were rising. We were losing land. There was no other place for students to go. The university had satellite campuses at Ertias Isle and Hierapolis--the deans left for those places--but there was no higher ground for the main institution. The Iron Bloods were left behind. Belo stayed, for Neena, I thought.

Professor Belo had survived the army's assault on the university and our faint resistance only to be struck by a pipe bomb while at the market buying her favorite cranberry and lemongrass tea at Hattie's stall. There was a part of me that wanted to take on some burden of guilt because the market was so near my house, and she might have been going to or from the university. Maybe if I had not volunteered our house, she would not have been there.

That was naught but a flash of egotism. The universe does not pay that much attention to me. It was a random act, yet the army could not have done themselves a better favor. There was no one so anathema to their cause as Professor Belo. She taught us Seasteaders that there was another way, that we did not have to obey soldiers or conventions and she gave us the tool to escape, a rust-resistant serum we could make with our Iron Blood.

~ 6 ~

BELO'S SEA-FAIRING

Even at age twenty-one, I experienced the tightening of time that happens as one grows old. I now considered Belo, who died at age 40, young. Although when I first took her classes, I would not have thought so. She had left her partner, Neena, clear instructions on how to eulogize her. Her family was there as well and many children.

A sea-fairing had been assembled. Belo's body was laid out before us. We Iron Bloods filed by her corpse. When the others retreated, I stayed nearby. I leaned over her body and took one of the coins from my pocket. I reached into her mouth and placed it under her tongue. The body she'd left behind felt spongy and unreal. Then it was hoisted atop the pyre.

Neena's grief seeped out from under her veil. She recited a poem she had written for Professor Belo about the sea.

Once blue water lived,
Now red waters rust,
No one can swim within,
What lies beneath? My love.

Timbol and Georgios spoke. Deuc, Merl, and Desiree were quiet.

"Belo was fascinated with the rust whales, sharks, and squid--how they had evolved and were able to withstand the corrosion. We wanted to know why all the smaller fish, the ones people once ate and survived off the plenty of the sea, all had died."

"Do you remember that salty food she served us once at a Seastead party?" I asked. "She would never say where it had come from."

We all remembered this now.

"I thought it was something I'd imagined. It was so different. Otherworldly," Timbol said.

I thought when Neena passed me that she would hand me another coin. I was just coming out of that age when I thought everything was about me. I felt that I had dreamed this moment. Maybe I had. In reality, she gave me nothing. Belo's rickety metal sea-fairing raft, a *mokol*, was pushed out of the harbor. As it floated out, I watched the flame along with everyone else and realized that life is long, but also may be short. The flames flickered blue and then out when they touched the metal. There was no precious wood to spare for a proper sea-fairing. Unless we grotesquely coated her body in a serum made of our own blood, her body would corrode, not burn.

I wondered if Neena thought this, too, and it added to her grief.

What projects had my professor been working on? What research would now go unfinished?

Later, I thought of my own predicament. Alex Belo had been my mentor. She knew best the quality of my work and now that knowledge was lost. If it had not been clear before, with the coming of the soldiers and the rising waters, it was clear now. I had no future. What my grandparents had feared and planned for, what my parents had run from, had come to pass. It had come for me. I had no place to run.

We gathered around and sang the sea-fairing song. As I watched the pyre float out to sea, its dull blue flames flickering, I remembered the underwater quality of Deuc's last song at Merops.

Before we left, Neena took Timbol and me aside. "Don't count me among your Seasteaders anymore. Keep me out of it. But she wanted you to have these."

She gave us both scrolls (precious, rare items written on real paper made of trees) and when we compared them later saw that I had the blueprints for the Seastead and Timbol the formula for the Iron Blood serum.

Belo's death brought the Seasteaders even closer. I became resolute. In order for higher knowledge to continue in the face of war, we had to create a place apart unbound by the previous conflicts, a fresh start. We had to build the Seastead. It was imperative.

Not long after Belo's death, what my father had most feared came to pass. After the soldiers commandeered the market--and all the high ground--they came for the Iron Bloods. They jailed the elders including my mother and her boyfriend, Reese, but there were also massacres of youth in the streets. The air smelled of iron and rust-stained grooves flowed between the cobblestones.

Rumors then spread that the soldiers were being disciplined for indiscriminate killing. We took a little hope from that until they rounded up us Iron Blood students. It wasn't the killing that Balor's army disliked. It was the waste of a precious resource--our blood.

The intelligence officers did not know of Belo's serum, but her work brought attention to us. They suspected us, well, our blood, of being useful. The time for academic discussions ended.

They made a prison out of Tillitat Manor. Marshall had disappeared-- jailed or killed we could not be sure. Neena wasn't with us. Her Iron Blood was secret. Georgios and Deuc were there. The brothers roomed upstairs in the West Wing with Timbol and Merl. Desiree and I stayed together in my grandmother's room near the kitchen.

She cooked the meager fare we had, mostly rice, nothing fresh.

Why didn't we fight? We were trapped, but we Seasteaders planned our escape.

They came often and drew our blood. It was the blood they wanted, fresh, untainted, healthy young blood. I knew all of the men and women imprisoned. I didn't know them well, but many of them from Merops and from the university. We watched each other and the soldiers watched us. Outside Tillitat, nervous soldiers killed citizens of Le Merde at random. We were kept safe because of what our blood could be worth--a means to hold back the rust. Our blood saved us. Professor Belo had taught them that, but they did not know Belo had already developed such a serum and Timbol held the recipe.

Held captive in my grandmother's house, the students of La Merde University had time on our hands. Desiree, Timbol, Merl, Georgios and I played many games of Cardinal, a card game imprinted with the four directions. It was a time of great risk, but also captivity and boredom.

I knew what the others were like from their card games. I had a sense of their strategy. Merl joked through the whole game and was terrible at bluffs, but he got excited when he was winning. The more he concentrated the worse off he was. When he just played loosely, he had natural luck and would win many games. He liked to gloat even when his hand was bad.

Desiree strategized carefully but would often toss all her plans away on a risky move. She either won or lost big. Desiree bluffed and did it well.

Timbol liked to bluff but was poor at it. He played a careful game, but he liked to use power moves. He'd get excited when he was winning and when losing would play it off as if he didn't care.

"It's just a game," he'd shrug.

I, of course, loved strategy. I'd plan out long plays many moves ahead and try to predict what the other players would do. Then someone like Georgios would see what I was doing and make a play to throw me off. Georgios liked to wait and strategize. He played the most like me.

I loved the game best though when one of my long plays came to fruition and I suspected that sometimes Georgios helped me even when it was to his own detriment. He, too, liked to see a slow plan come to success.

Deuc was the only one who didn't play. He practiced his music and kept apart.

On the anniversary of my grandmother's death, the soldiers who seemed more lax and distracted than usual, relented. Desiree and I had at first begged them daily to let us go to the market. When weeks dragged on without the fulfillment of that request, we'd asked them to restock our supplies and bring us some fresh food. We needed some lentils and greens to replenish our iron. We were all looking ghastly by now.

To our surprise, the soldier said, "Just go yourself. Get back directly or I'll be done with you and your friends will starve."

Surprised by our freedom, Desiree and I walked out on to the street. There was barely a path from my grandmother's house. It was terribly overgrown, and the ground was soggy. We sloshed through rust water puddles.

There were soldiers everywhere in the market and few items for sale. The vendors looked as battered as their produce. We walked past the narrow street where Merops had been, but the sign had been removed and the soldiers pressed against us and kept us from lingering.

We purchased some rice, greens, and stringy root vegetables and placed them in the basket. We were ready to return, and I could tell Desiree wanted to get home and cook some of what we had procured.

"I want to look for Hattie, the tea vendor," I said.

"We've got to get back," Desiree said. "You heard him."

"Yes, but it was nana's favorite." That might have softened her at any other time. She knew my grandmother by reputation in life and had certainly heard enough of my stories about her, living in grandmother's bedroom, but it was a fearful time.

"No. We can't take the time."

I was steering her through the market scanning for that familiar face. "She might have some spices too, if anyone would. She might have anise, even."

That had Desiree's attention. She loved anise in her beans and greens.

When I spotted Hattie, I tugged at Desiree's sleeve, and she followed me.

"Nata, I don't have that rose orange anymore," Hattie said. "The roses won't bloom. The air and the water's too acid for 'em now. The General's chased our traders to the south away. There's no citrus to be found. We'll all get scurvy."

She did have a bit of anise and cloves secreted away and she spared them for us. Desiree smiled and relaxed. There was no one like a smiling Desiree. She was serious mostly, but I understood the desire to please her for the reward of her smile.

Then a commotion broke out in the marketplace. There was shouting. A ratfin rushed by me and I snatched it up. The scared creature clawed its way into my arms and left a couple marks.

"We're getting rid of those vermin," said a passing soldier. "Orders. They are making people sick."

"It not them, it's the rising rust and the lack of food," Hattie said.

We walked by a pile of ratfin corpses.

I hid the one I'd caught in my basket beneath the leafy greens. Fortunately, it was a smart one and its instinct was to hide.

They hauled Hattie to her feet and began to drag her across the square. She caught my eye and winked.

I wanted to help her, but Desiree grabbed my arm, "We have to get back to the Seasteaders."

Then the ground beneath us shook and a boom sounded from the harbor. En masse the market seemed to move downhill toward the sound. It began to slide. A few of the vendors began to calmly gather a few wares and move higher, Desiree pulled that way too although there was only a tiny alpine forest above us. Maybe a few people could have undisturbed huts there, but there was no farmland, no future there. The soldiers all began to run downhill. They'd been spoiling for a fight and now it sounded like there was some action. Most of the people began to move toward the water. There was one ferry. It seemed the island was sinking now or about to be overrun by another invading force. It was time to leave.

My heart quickened with fear and anticipation. Finally!

I pulled Desiree into the flow streaming downhill. There was trampling, screaming, I saw Murine, the ratfin vendor's broken body, piled at the side of the road like one of her pets. There was no helping her.

Desiree and I veered toward Tillitat. No one had been using that path. The soldiers had kept everyone away from us. Perhaps, we'd been forgotten. When we arrived, we found just one soldier waiting.

When he saw us, he pointed his musket at us. Desiree and I stopped. "Good, you're back. I've been waiting."

"We said we would come back."

I knew this soldier. I remembered him from Merops. He'd asked me to dance once. I'd said no. I hadn't been friendly to him. He was a soldier and I was concerned about my own plans.

"Good. Good." He kept repeating the word. It made me nervous. Something was wrong.

"You're no good," he spat. "Your blood is worthless. All those tests. Nothing. Just pollution. That's what brought the plague down on us."

His face grew mean, but Desiree knew what he was about.

She held up the basket. "We got some greens, a little wilted, but I'll cook 'em up nice. We'll share them with you. You look a little thin."

We all did, us Iron Bloods more than most. Even Desiree's cheeks had lost their plumpness.

"We got some spices, too. Smell." She held the anise under his nose, and he inhaled.

"You've been told to kill us," I said, finally guessing. Desiree shot me a look. She'd known and was trying to make the soldier remember we were human. He was trying to talk himself into killing us.

I saw the look in his eyes. I saw him remember my rejection.

"You should have danced with me," he said.

"I guess I should," I said.

He hesitated, grim and angry, and then shook his head. "Nah, we were both at Merops. We were free to do as we liked. Or not. Look, I'm going. If I drown, I'll do it freely. Praise the Mountaintops! But Balor won't forget you. He'll come here or he'll find you. No place you can go anyway. I'll let someone else handle the mess."

"Thanks," I said sarcastically, but Desiree saved us again. She put his hand on his arm.

"What will you do? There'll be...discipline. Stay with us?"

"No. I'd be too ashamed to desert. I'm going to go high and take my chances. There's a few places up there. Maybe eke something out. Maybe I'll see you up there. Most everything near the water is gone."

With that, he finally lowered his gun and walked resolutely up the street.

~ 7 ~

SEASTEAD MEETING

Desiree and I ran up the stairs of Tillitat Manor. The house was empty, but when we yelled, "Seasteaders!" we heard a call from above. We unlocked the door to the attic and joined Timbol, Merl, Georgios and Deuc.

They had heard the boom of the landslide and after being shuffled into the attic by the soldiers had guessed what was coming next.

"That soldier was considering whether to kill us. Really talking himself up for it," Desiree said.

"Well, we would have made it difficult," Merl said. "Now what do we do? I suppose we go high and then try to launch our seastead."

Grandmother's attic smelled of rosewater, orange oil, and blood. I had imagined this meeting, this moment, when we would decide to undertake utopia, but I had thought it would be a leisurely discussion over biscuits and tea, not a hasty retreat from soldiers and chaos. I thought Professor Belo would lead us. Instead, there we were. There I was.

"I think it's already built," Deuc said.

"What?" I asked astounded.

"Belo, didn't have a chance to tell us, but I think she and your grandfather had a lot of things in motion. That blueprint you have is complete and once she had the serum...well," Deuc said.

I unscrolled the Seastead design. I stared at it to look busy, but I was intimately familiar with it: the circular rings, the platform, and the piers. Here was the kitchen. Here was the garden with the room for the raised beds, one for each passenger. Here the mechanics quarters. Up front the engine room. There were sailboats strapped to each side. These shaded patches were the solar panels. The lofted tower room would be mine, a place to get away. From the design, it did look ready and waiting for us.

"You think it's just out there?" I asked.

I didn't trust Deuc. I knew he'd act in his own interests, and I didn't know exactly what those were. He remained an enigma. It would have been simpler if Deuc were not with us. It would have been easier for me if I had not been distracted by the brothers.

"I helped her get a lot of iron out there," Deuc said.

Georgios gave him a look. "So, you've actually seen it?"

"No, but I think it's there," Deuc said.

"Well, there is a boat with a motor in my father's shed. It's a good-sized skipper already coated in the serum. So we'd have that. We could go somewhere else," Georgios said.

It didn't take a lot of time to decide. There wasn't much for us to disagree on at this point. We had to leave La Merde. Usually when we met, there was dissension. This time everyone was talking and agreeing faster than I'd ever experienced. We all wanted an excuse to set out for sea. We all wanted our seastead dream to begin to take shape. It had taken Belo years to convince the others to seastead. Then, when there was no option, of course, it took no time at all. The time for debate was over.

"We go here now," I said pointing at the scroll. "This is where the iron bloods will live."

"It will take all of us to make this work," Timbol said.

By work, he meant survive.

We would need Merl to purify the water, run the solar panels, and make repairs; Desiree and Timbol to grow the food and cook it;

Georgios to operate the platform and chart our way; Timbol to explore the depths; and all of us to bleed so we could coat the beams and keep the platform from corroding.

"We need to get seed," Desiree said.

It was decided that Georgios and Merl would raid the supplies before they left and get the boat hidden in Marshall's shed.

Timbol would get the lab materials and Desiree and I would gather up food.

"I'll get the serum," Deuc said.

None of our meetings ever went as smoothly again. That was the last time we'd be so quick and decisive.

I petted the ratfin snuggled against my neck. "You're safe, little survivor," I whispered to it.

"There's one more thing," I said. "I need to get my mother."

After a long silence, Deuc spoke. "Nata, the prison fell in the slide, into the sea. The soldiers said."

"They cheered," Merl said.

"My mother? Reese? My aunts?"

Georgios took my hand. "There's nothing we can do."

I let him embrace me, but then I pulled back.

"Neena, Professor Belo's widow, I can't leave without her."

Georgios gave me a look of concern, not disagreement but worry. Desiree looked surprised, but no one argued. They knew there was no point. It was clear from my voice, I was going.

"Fine, I can get the seed myself," Desiree said.

I gathered up my maps and plans and coins. We set out to do our own preparations. We'd meet at Marshall's.

I was afraid every minute I was separated from the seasteaders, from Georgios. I worried that we would not be reunited, but I was also excited. The blueprint for utopia had long been in my mind and here was an opportunity to test it.

The emigration line for the ferry off La Merde was packed. People holding packs, carpetbags, and the hands of wailing children waited in a warehouse just above the water line. The line looped back and forth. At the front, soldiers were taking tickets and searching bags and slowly, one at a time, people were boarding the last running ferry headed off the island.

It was a ferry just like the one I'd arrived on, and I wondered how far it would get before it sank. The people were headed for any available peak, the tops of another island, hoping to rejoin families long left behind. Those families would only be there if they were Peakers, people who had refused to leave. Anywhere these people were heading that was not overrun by Balor's men was not worth landing on and would likely soon be underwater.

I found Neena waiting near the end of a very long line. I hugged her.

"Dear Nata," she said. "It took me a long time, but I've decided to go. There's nothing for me here. Since I'm not an Iron Blood I can leave for another island."

Of course, I'd long since realized it was not true. Neena did have Iron Blood. It was what Professor Belo had used on her experiments, but the idea that she was not had kept her safe.

"Where will you go?"

She shrugged.

"Someplace. Where all these people are going."

"Some war-torn island, Neena? It won't be there very long."

"I have a ticket." She held up the pink stub. "And I have family on Iylla. I haven't seen them in a long time. They could be on a peak somewhere."

“Or you could come with me, with us. They are leaving the students alone now, the Iron Bloods.”

I could see the question in her eyes. I just gave her a pleading look wishing she could read my mind.

"Or you could come with me." She showed me her extra ticket, a withered slip. "They gave me Alex's. Forgot they killed her, I guess."

I remembered the journey to La Merde with my mother and how I'd thrown the dead ratfin overboard. I could escape, but to leave Georgios and Deuc. I would never do that. It was unthinkable.

"This family, they'll take you in?"

"Of course. They are family," she said, but she didn't sound excited about the possibility.

I didn't think I could convince her, so I just stood with her. I knew the Seasteaders would be getting impatient, but it was important to be with Neena for the time she had left. I just stayed beside her. While we were in that line, it was uncertain where we were going. Until a decision is made, every way is open.

I fantasized about stealing Neena's ticket so that she had no choice and had to come with us, but I didn't know what the Seasteaders' fate would be. As much as I felt it would be right for her to join us, I couldn't make that decision for her. I couldn't carry the burden of responsibility for her happiness if I were wrong.

We neared the front of the line and watched a family drama unfold. One of the children had lost a ticket. A mother and father were about to be separated. It was the father's family they were going to, so the mother would stay behind. "They'll be kinder to the children if you are there," she said.

I looked at Neena, crying for that family, and saw a way to get what I wanted.

So, I stole Neena's tickets and in slow motion I handed one to the mother.

Her eyes brightened. "Thank you." She hurried forward.

Someone saw though and there was an immediate clamor. There were not enough tickets to go around.

"They had an extra."

"Do they have another one?"

I handed the ticket back to Neena and I watched her press it into the nearest grubby hand without looking. She didn't want to make a choice either, to be responsible for anyone's fate. But she came with me.

When we got outside, I pulled her close. "We seasteaders are your family, too."

Then, I whispered the secret I hoped would make this all okay. The secret that I hoped was true.

"They built the Seastead. It exists."

"Alex's place." She stopped crying. "I hoped so. Oh, out on the water."

It was a surprise to her, not entirely, but enough that she hadn't feigned her reaction. Alex had had to keep the craft secret so the General wouldn't find it. Neena was a true lander who loved the earth and did not want to leave solid ground behind. She loved water as a poetic concept, but not as a homeland. Still, I didn't feel badly about deceiving her. I was that certain. She must have had an idea what alternative I was offering. I remembered what Professor Belo had said about where we were going, to leave it all behind. We would go to join the sea.

I took Neena's hand, and we made our way to Marshall's store. It had a warehouse connected to it just beside the water. Once, we would have called the body of water a bay. Now, the water had risen so high Marshall's was nearly in the ocean. Instead of the ocean being comfortably shaped around La Merde, La Merde was now settled uncomfortably in the ocean. The waters were rising. The soldiers, and anyone able, were fleeing the corrosive sea overflowing the island.

We found Georgios, Desiree, Merl, and Timbol staring down at a rusty metal raft like the one we'd sent Belo's corpse to sea on.

"Where's the boat?" I asked. Then, "Where's Deuc?"

Then I knew. Deuc had taken our boat.

"Why would he go without us?"

Now all of our prompt decision-making was undone. When we decided to go to the Seastead we weren't planning to fit six people on a sea-fairing *mokol.* The bottom of the raft looked hopelessly thin. The water around the house had soaked up through the concrete floor and we were lucky the *mokol* was stored upside down. The edges of it were soft and red. We didn't have any serum to coat the bottom with to shore it up. Once we were on the Seastead, we hoped, that there would be a lab where we could make more. We would each give our monthly donations of blood to create it and use it to upkeep the platform. That was the hope. Like everything else, it was really a drowning hope, but it was what we had. We had to push off into the sea.

"Where would Deuc have gone?" Desiree asked. "The only place to go is the Seastead, maybe, and why would he go without us."

"He needs us," Timbol said.

"Well, we'll shore it up with some boards," said Georgios, beginning to look around the bay for any wood. "And hope it lasts long enough."

"We've got these," Desiree said, holding up two sets of oars.

"We'll need those to row."

"That's what I meant."

"It will be slow going," Neena said. "Will we even make it before..."

Merl cut her off. "Hell, yes. Give me one of them oars."

Georgios tore his father's house apart looking for wood.

"Long ago these houses were made of wood when it was plentiful. It might be that there's a remnant under the walls, some overlooked scrap," he said. He found a piece of plywood in the bathroom beside the tub. It was somewhat soft itself, but it might buy us time.

When the *mokol* was as fortified from the corrosive sea as we could manage with such haste, we hesitated on the shore reluctant to leave the land until Merl urged us onward.

"This is no time to back down," Merl said. "Go on."

Together, we pushed out into the water over the sand. Then Georgios, Merl, Desiree, Timbol, Neena and I all climbed onto the rocking *mokol,* just skimming above the sea under our weight.

Did I mention that none of us knew how to swim? No one did in Pacifica at that time. It was an art lost when the waters grew red and blistered the skin and killed the smaller sea creatures.

Part Two: Death

~ 8 ~

PADDLING OUT

We Seasteaders were finally leaving the land behind us. There was hardship ahead, but also a chance to change the world. An individual can make an impact, but not without sacrifice. Sometimes, the sacrifice means giving up objects and ideas that were never a boon to begin with, other times it's a loss of independence, privacy, and autonomy. I have learned that some of my most dearly held treasures were more valuable when dropped into the ocean and sunk to the bottom of the sea.

"Is change worth the sacrifice, when the loss is love and liberty?" I've asked myself. On a trajectory to change the world, there's not much choice.

The Seasteaders left shore on a rickety *mokol.* In some ways it made sense that we were using a sea-fairing craft, we also meant to make a one-way trip. There would be no coming back to the island, to La Merde, to the ruins of the university, to Octavia Street, to my grandmother's home, to the market filled with good things to eat, or to Merops. We were leaving behind all the places we knew, and we could not be sure that the Seastead existed. We knew only the plans for it, the dreams, and the ideals. How and when would the university and Professor Belo have had the opportunity to build the platform? We only hoped that the Seastead would be there. What is hope, but a hook?

"We've been working on the details," Merl said. "That says something. Filtration systems, food, water pumps. That says something was in place."

We all liked that he said this. It sounded logical and true, but I think all of us harbored doubts, except perhaps for Georgios. When I asked him later though, Georgios said he did not doubt.

"Of course, my father and Belo built it," he said. "Marshall would do anything for his sons and Alex wanted to see her vision realized."

I had some ideas, but I kept them to myself. We were scared enough. That was the moment I learned to keep my ideas to myself, at times a necessary skill.

Everyone looked at Neena, thinking she must have had some clue as Belo's intimate, but eventually we stopped pestering her with insistent glances.

"She didn't let me in on it," Neena said. "I can't believe it either. Maybe she was going to leave me. I felt we were growing distant. She spent more time at the school. She was buried in her research."

"Or she was busy building the Seastead," Merl said.

It struck me that the source of Neena's sadness, was the only hope for us. Please let Belo have been preoccupied with building the Seastead.

For now, all we could do was dip our oars into the rusty water, hope, and row toward the location indicated on the blueprint. The corrosive sea dripped off the ends of the oars and it wasn't long before the silver metal tips of the oars began to slide into the water. Dark blotches appeared on the oars' surface with jagged edges where holes were beginning to form.

Merl and Desiree started out rowing. At their best, they had both been strong: Merl from lifting pipes and digging trenches for the water flows and Desiree from lifting boxes and kneading bread. But we were all weak now from the bloodletting. Our arms were matchstick thin and the waves were thick, the sea was rough. We made slow progress. We followed the coordinates out to sea stroke by stroke as the sun dropped low in the sky.

"It's not too far, really," Timbol said.

"Oh, yeah, then take a turn," said Merl.

The *mokol* lurched over the sea and the iron spray stung our eyes. Timbol put on goggles, but we weren't all so well equipped and our eyes grew red.

The rust red water rose and dipped in the dusk. The setting sun cast a redundant rose light over the ocean waves. Amid it, we felt the sea's poisoned lifelessness. We could just see the ferry departing from La Merde heading south toward Scylla while we headed north. It threw more waves our way.

"I could be on that," Neena said. She sounded wistful and was.

"I gave you a choice," I snapped.

"Least you could have done," Neena said. "I'm not sorry now. I'm just scared."

"It's mostly soldiers, anyway," Timbol said.

The blue uniforms ringed the deck of the ferry. I wondered about the mother and daughter we'd given Neena's tickets to, had they even made it on board? Had they been permitted to go?

"Praise the mountains," Desiree said. "I'm glad you're with us, Neena, and I hope they find their way."

"Ha, praise water," Merl scoffed. "We may as well honor what's all around us."

We were now far out at sea and could no longer see La Merde, the weathervane on top of Tillitat Manor, or the distant ferry departing. I looked down at the pinkish bottom of the mokol. The rust-colored water was seeping up under the piece of soft board, turning it a pale pink. I imagined what the underneath of the *mokol* must look like: bubbling and sizzling in the Rust Sea, dark spots with jagged edges, thin beyond belief. I clutched the side of the boat only to feel the softening side, spongy, and wet beneath my hand. I wiped the pink froth of the corroding boat on my pants. My hand stung slightly from the rust touch.

"Who's scared? Let me row again," Merl said, and dug his oar in. "Row, row."

Georgios relieved Timbol and I was reassured to feel the boat surge forward. Georgios was stronger than he looked. If he'd been as strong as his will, he would have been a leviathan. We would have been to the middle of the ocean in two strokes.

As the water rose, those of us who weren't rowing watched our boots and tried to keep them out of the water, squatting high in the center of the raft, and pressing our feet up under our behinds.

Those who were rowing looked ahead and Timbol gauged our progress on the compass. For the longest time, we stared at a blank horizon filled with red. Then a blotch appeared in front of us with jagged edges marring the round red sun.

"There," Georgios said.

There looked to be metal struts rising into the beet red sun. I had never seen a structure like this so sharp and angled and created of metal. Most of the buildings and objects I was familiar with were made of curved lines of wood, which resisted the corrosive sprays, but was in short supply. The struts were the color of dried blood. It was in fact our own dried Iron Blood which coated the struts so that they could resist the sea spray. At the top rose a weathervane, just like on top of grandmother's house. Our blood was our salvation. Our blood would save us from the Rust Sea.

"She did it. Without me. Oh, Mother..." Neena said.

I didn't catch the last word. I think it was "useless."

"She did it with you," Merl said. "That's your blood, be sure of it."

As he said it, a huge spray of water rushed over the boat. At the same time, the *mokol* shook and a thunk hit the side. An arch of red water soaked us. While we hurried to wipe it off and protect our eyes, something swiped the other side of the raft.

"Merl!" Georgios called.

Merl was no longer on board. A fin rose out of the water. It was black, oily, and rust red. It was covered in a thick crust of boils raised by the corrosive sea. Merl bobbed in the waves beside the fin.

"Shark!" Timbol said.

I knew there were still some of these creatures in the water reportedly seen around islands where General Balor and his soldiers had held some of their bloodiest battles. They trailed behind Balor's ships eating waste. But what were they doing here? What was there to eat besides us?

Georgios leaned way out over the water and reached down into it with an unprotected hand.

"No!" I yelled, but then I saw him come up with the end of an oar. He swung it out to Merl. Merl grabbed the end of it and we helped haul him in. His skin was red. It would turn black and bleed.

A second strike hit the boat. There was a long-ridged plank surfacing on the other side of the boat away from the fins. I'd seen at least three fins at once rising out of the water. I wasn't counting, but I felt surrounded. There were rust sharks on one side with the *mokol* battered in between and its five scrawny Iron Blood occupants.

We clung to the sides of the boat. I felt the sponginess in my hands again. I pushed Neena into the center of the raft. The ratfin scrabbled against my neck as the *mokol* rocked.

"Hunker down," Timbol shouted.

I looked up at the platform. The distance to it was not far: a few fathoms. We could have swum there if the water had been clean and free of beasts, and if anyone in Pacifica knew how to swim. We had stopped rowing to concentrate on staying in the boat while creatures thumped against it. I imagined the bottom breaking apart. I felt the sides slipping under my hands. We waited listening to the sharks thump against the *mokol*.

Georgios was the first to pick up an oar again. "Row, row, row!"

Timbol dug in. We made it to the metal ladder that rose up to the platform. I sent Neena up first, then Desiree, clanging. Timbol, Georgios, and I hoisted Merl up. His skin burned. It was reddened, raised, and threatening to slough off. He screamed as we manhandled him, but we got him aboard. The *mokol* stayed on the water to sink with the circling sharks. The sharks would always be there. This part of the sea was their home, too.

There was also a whale, she with the big, wet, red-rimmed inky eye surrounded by fat, oily, black barnacles. We had arrived at the Seastead as promised, as hoped, but we were not alone.

~ 9 ~

ARRIVING ON THE SEASTEAD

I did not expect the Seastead to be paradise. We'd lived our lives in fear of the encroaching water, with water ever on our minds, but we were not of the water. On the water was a discomfiting place.

Now, what we'd run from, the water, surrounded us. It was to be our home. It offered a fearful kind of freedom. We could do whatever we liked with no thought for anyone else's laws or hierarchies. We were free from Peaker philosophies, General Balor's orders, and soldiers' battles. We were all on equal ground here--what little of it there was.

The platform was the size of grandmother's living room. It was cold grey metal with a thick crust of applied blood on the surface. The middle of it was flat, square, and open like a courtyard or the deck of a barge. It was raised on a float and struts rose from the sides. Along each side there were rooms and glass windows. There were metal stairs up to the second deck and on the north side one more thin set of stairs to a small room at the top, a lookout. It was shaped like a square compass with a weathervane affixed to its highest point.

Merl lay on the deck, breathing heavily, panting. He stared up.

"That's for me," he said, claiming the loft on arrival with his skin burning in his weakened state.

The Seastead looked just as its blueprint. I began to search for the things I expected to see. The ground floor garden with eight two-by-four-foot raised beds was there. Green shoots were already sprouting from the soil.

We were all exhausted from rowing and it was dusk now headed towards dark, but we were excited. The Seastead was our dream and now our hard reality.

Desiree was drawn to the garden. She examined the tiny greens. “There's onions, garlic, spinach, and tomatoes already growing. And there's an herb garden in the kitchen."

"Below there will be a boiler room," I said.

The Seasteaders began to explore their piece of paradise.

"It is not paradise," I reminded myself, speaking aloud.

"But it's here," Georgios said inspecting the bloodied sides of the platform which seemed to resist the Rust Sea's corrosion.

Timbol stared over the side at the sharks. "Why are they here? What's the food source?"

"I'm sure they are drawn by all the blood paint on this thing. It's layered on, but its flaking off. We'll need to recoat it soon."

"And we're lower down than the plans call for, closer to sea level," Timbol noted.

Georgios turned from where he was inspecting the sides of the platform.

"What are we going to do for Merl?" Neena whispered to me. His skin was beginning to blacken. We did not have much in the way of medicines. Nothing to heal burns like those.

"Let's look around," I said.

Desiree was exclaiming over the kitchen, "There's refrigeration and a freezer and there are lights."

Curtains with lace frills framed the window looking out to the deck. The light shone over Merl's prostrate body. There were herbs in the cupboard, but nothing potent for healing.

Neena searched the room next door, and we heard her cry out, "There's a library and my books are in it."

The poetry anthologies she loved and copies of her own chapbooks, "The Rust Garden" and "Sea Hands," were on the shelves.

I put my arm around her, "Alexandra clearly planned this for you. She meant for you to be here one day."

"She did," Neena said. "And, but for you, I almost didn't come."

I thought of how sad I would have been to see those books without Neena and was glad I had gone after her.

Professor Belo had clearly planned this place for all of us. There were maps laid out on a table in Georgios' room and in a room upstairs on the bed there was another coin for me. This was number three. I picked it up and put it in my pocket. It felt good to claim a space, a room, with a door, and put down my few possessions.

Then I went outside and leaned over the railing at Timbol, "Nice digs?"

"Solar panels up there," Merl groaned.

"Yep, charts of the weather," Timbol said. "The gear rooms are below. Come take a look."

Timbol, Georgios, and I descended with a soft clang, the sound of movement on the Seastead, which would become so familiar.

"I found a supply room," Georgios said holding up a pair of goggles. Inside were gloves, goggles, rubber boots, hats and pants: the equipment we would need to maintain the Seastead and in case of storms.

There was a keg that had been filled with Iron Blood serum. Its sides were crusty with dried blood, but there was only sludge in the bottom.

"We'll need to replenish this soon. Timbol, can you make the serum?" I asked.

"I think so," he said.

We found no medical supplies and there was no sign that the Seastead had been occupied.

"Georgios, where's Deuc?" I asked. "I thought he'd be here."

Georgios shrugged. "I don't know. I thought so, too."

The basement was dark. Filled with a soft purple light and there was a soft, trickle of water and a bubbling sound.

"The boiler's here and the serum," Georgios said. "But what to make of this, Timbol?"

Along the far side of the room under a UV light was a hydroponic garden. The leaves growing within were a deep, nutritious green and there were ripe, bright red round hanging fruits, tomatoes, and strawberries. The water in the tank was clear and beautiful. The white roots of the plants swayed in it. A faucet above the trough let out a steady stream of clear water.

"Where's it coming from? Where's the filter?"

"I don't see anything," Timbol said. "It's trickling in from out there."

"From the Seastead deck? It's been a long day," Georgios said. "Maybe we're missing something, we're tired. Let's think about it tomorrow. We need Merl."

I wanted to go back upstairs to that quaint kitchen. We were all tired. We just wanted to feel safe, but it was clear it might be a long time before that happened, if ever.

We heard steps on the landing. Desiree descended carrying a glass of something clear.

"Guys! Check this out," she said. She held up the glass to Georgios, "Taste."

Georgios took it.

"Be careful," I said.

He drank. "Water? What makes water taste like that?"

He passed the glass around and we all exclaimed. It was so fresh and clean and sweet. I'd never had or seen water that was so clear before. We usually drank filtered water, and it was always a pale pink or yellow with traces of metal.

"It came right out of the kitchen tap," Desiree said.

"Let's take this up to Merl," I said.

We all went up except Timbol who could not leave a mechanical mystery alone, especially one that could be key to our survival. I held the glass to Merl's lips. He drank tentatively at first and then deeply. He lay back and rested.

"I've got to see the filter," he said.

"I found some lotion, too." Neena said. "A big vat of it in the closet in my room."

The women smeared it on our faces and necks. It smelled of roses. I wished I could have brought my grandmother here. Of course, she never would have left her home, but now, with nowhere better to go, and with the Seastead so clearly stocked and supplied with us in mind it felt luxurious. The lotion soothed my acid raw skin. Georgios took some for his hands.

"How does this feel?" Neena dabbed some on Merl's raw skin.

"Tingles," he said. "Nice."

His skin looked better. Neena applied it lightly gently to his face, arms, and legs. Then she carefully peeled his shredded shirt over his head and rubbed it over his torso.

We sat beside Merl listening to his ragged breaths become calmer as the scent of roses wafted toward the stars.

"I'll make us some dinner," Desiree said. "There's a store of corn flour upstairs and I'll harvest some of those tomatoes."

Just then there was a horrible clank. The Seastead shuddered and metal ground. The grinding carried on. It felt like the Seastead was ripping apart.

"The floor's moving," Desiree said.

"I found a switch," Timbol said.

"So, you touched it?" Georgios said, accusingly.

The middle of the platform was opening, a large square in the center. It was dark on the deck and what was under the metal was just as dark, but shiny. The moonlight shone down, and we saw the waves. This was the only land we had and now it was tearing apart and showing more water.

The ratfin buried into my shoulder.

"This wasn't part of the plan," Timbol said.

"Don't touch the water," I said.

The pool sparkled like a dark jewel. A fresh scent rose off of it. There was a pool at the center, and we could see stairs leading into the water and some dark shapes to the side. They looked like the heads of some sea creature. But the smell that rose from the pool was sweet and it was clearly the source of the water we'd drank in the kitchen and the water that swelled the tomatoes in Desiree's hands. The water shone. The ratfin scurried down my shoulder. It sniffed and drank in the water and then entered it gliding across the surface with its fins outstretched. Then it slipped under.

"Georgios, ratfin!" I lurched forward but hesitated to enter the water.

Georgios plunged in, he could not swim, but he lashed out and he soon had the ratfin in his hands.

I ran down the steps. The water was warm, and I reached for Georgios and then Timbol was beside me. Together we caught Georgios' hand and pulled him to the steps where the water was shallow.

"Be careful, there's a bit of a current. But the water is fresh and warm and sweet."

I grabbed Georgios a blanket and he returned the ratfin to my neck. The ratfin nuzzled against my neck and I looked into its bright eyes.

"That's twice you've been saved. I'm going to call you In-fin."

We stared at the pool and stared. Desiree broke the spell.

"OK, I'm starving," she said, and then wandered back to the kitchen. Eventually, we all trailed after her, exhausted with our thoughts.

That night we stayed up late and gathered in the kitchen. We ate polenta with a thick tomato sauce, and we drank glasses of the water, which streamed freely from the tap.

Remembering the keg of rust-blood serum, I realized we perhaps could have saved the *mokol.* But where would we go? This Seastead was our best hope now.

"It was wasteful about the raft. We just let it sink," I said.

"I never want to be on it again," Neena said.

"We couldn't spare the blood for it anyway," said Timbol. "This whole vessel will need to be recoated soon and there's only the six of us--and we're all pretty drained."

By the time we were ready for sleep, Merl was well enough to climb up to his loft at the top of the Seastead. His lotion-coated skin was looking better, pinker and smoother.

Timbol took a room in the basement. Neena and Desiree stayed up talking. The rooms they took were on the main floor by the kitchen and library. Georgios stood with me beside the pool, and we listened to Merl clanging away in the mast, Timbol shuffling below, Desiree and Neena's chatter and the sounds of them nesting away the few items we had brought with us, tucking our few seeds and supplies into the cabinets and shelving our few books alongside the ones already supplied.

"OK, I'm to bed," Georgios said.

"I'll just be a moment," I said.

The pool in the middle of the platform mesmerized me. Why was it here? What did it mean? Moonlight shone on the surface. A faint smell of cinnamon that reminded me of grandmother's tea wafted from the surface. I saw a gleam on a ledge below and I was certain it was yet another one of the coins meant for me shining underwater. I watched at first without getting close.

I walked around the pool and stepped closer to it to get a better look. Ripples moved across the surface of the pool starting out from the center. Bubbles rose up from the center and the water began to froth. I ran down the stairs unwary of the noise. I searched for the panel.

"Close it. Close it," I said.

Timbol came out and flipped the switch to shut the lid and close the hatch to the pool. The clanging shook the platform, but I could feel the shift in movement. The metal was scrolling back, cranking into place.

He held me in his arms.

"I'm afraid of what's below," I said.

"It's OK, we're all jangly now," he said. "It'll take some time to adjust, to feel safe."

Would I ever feel safe with all this water around me?

I was slow to ascend the stairs, nervous about what I would find. The floor closed slowly. It was just a quarter of the way across. The center of the pool was still. I thought I saw a movement below a seal shape.

Desiree was standing on the deck watching it close. "What's up?"

"Just keeping the rust out of there."

"Mmm," she said. "Let's not open and close that all the time. Makes a racket."

"Sure," I assented, unsure if I ever wanted to see it open again. We could just use the water and not wonder at the source. I laughed. It was a nervous laugh. Of course, that was impossible.

Above me, Merl was looking down over the mast, staring down at the platform. From his vantage point looking down into the pool, I wondered what he had seen.

Under the roof I felt a plunk, plunk, plunk like something was knocking on the door asking to be let in. It shook the platform, but that first night, for all we knew, it might have just been the lapping of waves.

~ 10 ~

MULIAN ARRIVAL

The next morning it was clear and calm for our first spring day at sea. For breakfast, Desiree made us hot corn mash with strawberries. Merl was mostly healed this morning, so it looked as though the burns were not as bad as we had thought when we brought him aboard. We ate heartily. The strawberries popped with sweetness. We were on our own at last, living the plans we had made over the past three years. Everyone but me was eager to look into the pool.

Sometimes, I wondered what would have happened if my mother had not left my father and we had stayed on Vancouver Island. I would not have condemned her to that, but still I wondered. Would the beatings have become progressively worse until he killed her? Surely that was what she had feared although it was hard to imagine such acts of violence from a family member and far easier to imagine it from the soldiers. Maybe she would have lived longer, nonetheless. What if I had never entered Merops and met Deuc and Georgios?

If I hadn't gone to university then playing at building utopias would have remained a childhood game. Much later, I would wonder what it would have been like if I had stayed longer with my companions on the Seastead. Would we have had children? Would I have died with them around me at age 91 like my grandmother? After we looked down into the pool, everything would be different, but there was no way for us to live without looking. For that, we would have had to be an entirely different kind of people, raised in a different place.

I was afraid, not just of what was in the water and where it came from, not just because I always imagined the worst, which always seemed a valid method of planning. It seemed to me the better prepared you were for defeats, the less likely they were to happen. I was more afraid because clean, pure water--an entire perfect pool of it--was a treasure, something to protect. Once we had something of worth to others, I would become afraid. Without the pool, there was no reason for anyone to try and find the Seastead. With the pool, they had reason and that meant an increased probability that they (soldiers or pirates) would find us. Soldiers, of any kind, were unlikely to be our friends.

There were so many things we could have done that first day. We had so much to do. We had to make our own food, clothing, and power. Neena could write. Merl could begin work on the boat he was already dreaming of building. Desiree could harvest seeds. I wanted to assign us tasks and begin to plan yet further ahead. I also wondered where Deuc was and wanted to take Georgios aside and ask him what he thought. However, we had arrived in our future plans at the very moment in which we foresaw no future. It was the perfect time for fate to intervene.

First, we had to drain blood and re-coat the vessel. We hoped Timbol would be able to recreate the serum. It was a question crucial to our survival which had to be answered.

At breakfast, we discussed who was able to give blood. Neena had been drained the longest of any of us so we decided to give her a rest, also Merl to give him time to heal, and Timbol to give him a better chance to think clearly. Myself, Georgios, and Desiree would give after we ate. I thought the loss of blood was adding to my irritability and nervousness, but there was no way around it.

In the light of day, the platform felt less solid than it had at night. The blood flaked off the struts and floated to the deck in the breeze. I would feel better when a fresh coat of rust protectant had been applied. We all would. I thought again that it might have been prudent to keep the small raft. Damn Deuc for leaving us without the boat. We were trapped on the water, barely afloat.

After breakfast, while everyone drank tea and looked over the railing at the ocean, spotting sharks, Merl took me aside. "Did you see something? Something that made you close the cover?"

"No," I shook my head. "Well, movement, maybe."

"Like a fish?"

"Bigger."

After tea, we drained blood so that Timbol could begin trying to resurrect the serum. He went below and began work.

Then they wanted to examine the pool. Merl went down to flip the switch and I stood next to Georgios holding his hand. There was that heavy clank. The rickety platform shifted. The grey metal floor ground aside revealing silvery waves. The water was bright, and it stretched endlessly below. Shining sliver and blue tiny fishes such as I had never seen darted through the sunlit pool. There was nothing in the center, just clear water infused with light. It looked to spiral down. Now I could see clearly, the ledge around the edge of the pool. It was four feet below around the outside and just wide enough to stand on. I saw the glint of the coin. I saw the familiar imprint of it. On the other side, were masks, strange inhuman looking masks.

We stepped into the water. It was warm and pleasant. No one felt anything strange except that we were in water, and it did not burn, it caressed our skin. Georgios stood beside me in the water. Desiree and Neena sat on the side and swung their legs in the water. Only Merl refused to go in. He was still scared from his plunge into the ocean on our way over.

"It feels soft. It might soothe your skin," Neena said.

"Nah, I've had enough of water, save for drinking," he said.

Instead, he walked over to examine the masks from the platform.

Desiree jumped into the water, onto the ledge and began to walk around. Then the current caught her, she swayed, yipped, and slipped from the ledge. Her head went under. Georgios leaned out and caught her hand.

There was a horrible moment when I thought the swirling current would pull them both under and then another horrible moment when Georgios heaved Desiree to him and onto the ledge.

I saw Georgios holding wet, shining Desiree and how quickly he'd reached out to meet her and I had a premonition. I knew then that they shared a connection. Yet, probably, nothing would happen between them so long as I was there.

Georgios stayed beside me while I reached down for the coin on the ledge. I had to fight the current to come up with it. Georgios caught my other hand to help me resist the current spiraling toward and pull me up. The coin was the same as my other coins. It was a sign. A direction.

"Let me see," Merl said, and I passed the thing to him. For the first time, I felt we Seasteaders had no secrets.

He twisted it and watched the coin flex. "OK, these creepy things are organic, a lot like these masks. They look kind of like some sort of helmet," Merl said. "They have a grey metallic sheen, but a rubbery softness."

Timbol had come up from below and he also leaned down to inspect and touch the masks.

"Rubbery. There are these hard nubs and soft tendril things. Yep, definitely organic, " he said, agreeing with Merl's assessment.

They smelled of kelp and sea salt, although this water was not salty.

While we examined them, the water began to froth and churn. We backed out of the water onto the Seastead deck.

"Should I shut it?" Timbol asked.

"Yes, shut it!" I directed.

"Let's see. Let's see," Georgios said.

We were planners, not the kind of people who reacted quickly to changing circumstance. I thought of utopias, I imagined the worst, but I wasn't prepared to fight it. None of us had a weapon stouter or more deadly than a wooden oar.

Merl picked up the oar.

It happened slowly. The bubbles rose. A crown appeared--that's what it looked like to us--lavender spikes adorned the head. Beneath that a lumpy visage. There were no facial features to fix on to. I could not discern eyes, nose, ears, or a mouth in that flakey, undulating, blue-green luminescent face. There was a short beard of tendrils and tentacles. A long silvery robe swirled around the rest of the long body, from the end of its beard for a length of at least seven feet to wherever it ended. We could not see its feet.

Perhaps it was the being's smell, foreign but spicy and sweet, of kelp and cinnamon, or maybe it was their stance and bearing, non-threatening yet confident. There was something about this being that made me regard it sympathetically as though it were myself. I wondered where it had come from and whether it had tired from its journey. Whatever it was, it was easily apparent to me that this strange creature was human, human in a way that the soldiers on the streets or even my father, when he had struck my mother, had not been. I felt at peace in their presence and then I began to feel excited. Anticipation welled up in me: What next?

The being made a low hum, a rhythmic churning came from them, and I wished we had Deuc with us, our musician. Music, not words, seemed the right way to communicate with this unusual being.

Then Neena, our poet, spoke:

"The sea, the fish, the tree, tree, tree;
Some rise, some seek, some be, be, be."

It was a simple poem, but the rhythm was right.

The emissary was pleased, I imagine. They turned to Neena and their beard and hair waved at her. He began to glide up the steps toward us. There was no up and down motion as he ascended just a gentle rocking. When he turned, we saw the twisted ropes that hung down his head and shoulders and swung heavily.

Later, I would know that the robe he wore was alive, a living shell with fluid movement, that the kingly crown was made of living shells as well, tubular shaped spikes filled with muscles. I would know that he moved on a soft muscular pod like a snail and beneath his robe his upper body was draped in cilia, and he both ate and loved with a thick trunk like appendage that came out of his side and was surrounded by eight thinner tentacles, which served as his arms, hands, and fingers. His lower body was coated in scales and rises of barnacle and that, among his kind, these creatures clung only to the best regarded Mulians. Abrador was highly respected. I would come to know Abrador intimately in all his strange nature.

It was good we did not know all that at the time--we who knew so little of the sea and who had grown up in fear of it.

Later he would tell me, "I went to greet you because I am to you, we think, the most unusual looking of Mulians, by far the most disturbing. After me, we thought, you would find the others less so, somewhat comforting. Until, that is, you went down and met the great ones."

At first glance, the emissary seemed strange, but not too strange after all we'd been through. While we feared the monotony and uncertainty of our precarious position at sea on the platform, his appearance gave us a future to focus on, a problem to solve, and questions to ask. What is life without questioning? Without mystery and puzzles?

In response to Neena, our visitor made more sound. He keened like a Rust Whale. He sang a greeting that sounded distant and muffled as if we were all underwater.

Beneath the sounds, I could feel words.

"Exiador," which meant welcome. I saw the word in my mind and felt it and recognized it from the imprint on the coins.

"They want to teach us," I said. "To swim and...I don't know, other things."

"They?" Merl asked.

"A name: Mu-lee-anns. Sea teachers. More teachers will come."

Abrador left us gifts: green algae lotion and a cinnamon and kelp-scented liquid that no one was anxious to try. These new supplies added to our stores.

He left the gifts and sank back below. Before we met another Mulian, we would have other visitors.

We would tend to the painting of the platform with our blood leaning far over the sides of the ship where the Rust Sharks swam and hanging below to get to the underbelly. It seemed to be holding up well enough.

Weeks later, Merl shouted down from the crow's nest, "A ship."

We looked out to sea and saw the galleon approaching flying a flag no one recognized.

"At least it's not Balor," I said.

"You'd rather the devil you don't know?" Timbol said.

"This time I'll take it," I said. "Shut the hatch. We don't want them to notice the water."

It closed with a clanking and the whole Seastead shook, but the motion was hidden in the ocean wind and waves. When the ship arrived, we did not get the devil we did not know. Apparently, we knew too many devils.

~ 11 ~

ELATHIAN RIPTIDERS

In making our Seastead plans, everyone had been envious of the Elathian Riptiders. They were a tight clan of craftsmen who had banded together early on when the water began to rise. No one knew how the pirates had been so prescient and certain. They had hoarded wood for themselves, and they had planned to be afloat, while everyone else clung desperately to the land and fought over it. They had planned and planted and cut down trees before the soil was too wet for the hard woods to grow and the land became too soft for their roots. They had moved animals with them onto the water as well. It was rumored that they had a large and well-defended floating island to the West.

The gleaming galleon that came toward us was made of mahogany and cypress. It had planks of red and gold. It had strong, solid flanks and cannons. The flag they flew was a tree with its roots exposed. No doubt, these were the legendary Riptiders who had hoarded wood and left everyone else behind to drown.

It was alarming to see the galleon bearing down on us. It was taller than an island top and lined with guns. We had the pool, our blood, and our meager supplies to protect and no means to do so. The ship towered over us.

"We didn't make any plans for defense?" Desiree said.

"Did you?" I asked.

"Well, even if we had weapons, would you use them or expect me to use them?" Timbol said.

"No, there's no reason for anyone to end up dead sooner than we will anyway," I said.

No, we hadn't made provisions to fight. Our goal had always been to prevent suffering and there was no weapon on earth that could alleviate that. Maybe that was why the earth had to be abandoned. The galleon pulled up beside us and lowered a plank down to our Seastead. Three men descended. One of them was Deuc.

"I thought we'd have more time before we were found," Merl said.

"Deuc," Georgios said. "He brought the pirates."

Deuc was with the Riptiders. He came down after the tallest of them, a dark-haired man who looked like he'd been long at sea, who stood and walked with a swagger of authority, and his brother who had reddish hair and a thin beard and more of a swing in his step than a swagger. Beside the pair, Deuc looked trivial in stature. His delicate features and playful curly hair made him seem like a toy. If I'd had any sense of survival, I'd have turned all my attention to these stout men, but in that moment, as always, Deuc held my full attention. I told myself I was incensed by his betrayal. In truth, I was excited to see him, and I wanted his attention, too. The men were armed with worn-looking pistols and swords, which they wore like their leathers. Deuc had a sword too, but it was too long for him and looked like decoration. I went right up to him and spewed words without thinking.

"You took our boat to the Riptiders. We barely made it out here on the raft. Merl fell in. There were sharks."

"Shush," said Timbol.

The more I spoke the angrier I became. I went from cold fear to hot fury in two seconds as soon as Deuc spoke. "I'm sorry I left you, but you wouldn't listen."

"Wouldn't listen to what?"

Deuc was always remembering conversations we hadn't had. It seemed we were always arguing about arguments I couldn't remember. He came at problems from a different tack. He would hear my words differently.

"I mentioned Riptiders and you shut me down," he said.

Then I did remember, a snippet. He'd mentioned Riptiders and I'd said, "OK, but we need to focus on the Seastead." Then, he'd been sullen, and I had talked to the others. So, that was the moment he'd made his own plan. That long ago.

"You never said you knew them, and you were going to take our boat," I said. "We didn't even know if the Seastead would really be here."

He looked chagrined for a moment. He did always look apologetic, when he bothered to apologize, on the rare occasions he felt it was required.

"Oh, right. Yes, I know, and I left you just that raft. That was terrible. I'm sorry," he said. "But I knew Georgios would make it out here." Then he turned to Merl. "You should see what they have. It's larger than any floating market. There are stairs and layers. There are cities afloat. The engineering..."

"Sure, they did all that, so they make their own laws, use all the wood, and screw the rest of us," said Timbol, but Merl looked interested.

Deuc shrugged. "It's like us at Merops. It's a sanctuary."

"This is our sanctuary," I said. "You plan to plunder it."

"Do I hear welcome aboard?" asked the tall Riptider. His beard tapered below his chin and had a curl to it on the end. There was a little grey in it. It looked a little alive, like the Mulian Abrador's beard, but it blew in the breeze, and it was made of human hair not seastuff.

Until now, the Riptiders had been standing over us, looking around the deck, taking inventory. They mostly hadn't reacted to my outburst. The elder one raised a wry smile.

"There's plunder is there?" He looked around and raised an eyebrow.

Of course, he couldn't see the pool. But could we keep him from noticing the tap water?

The younger one was eyeing Desiree and looked like he might be having other ideas about plunder. To my chagrin, Desiree was meeting his gaze. We'd been away a while and although Timbol, Merl, and Georgios were all rather attracted to Desiree, no one thus far had done more than appreciate her cooking. Georgios and I were the only couple. The others were afraid to disrupt their friendship on the tiny, uncertain platform. Romance would happen in time.

"I'm sorry for our rudeness," Georgios said, stepping forward. "We were surprised to see Deuc. Can I show you around?"

"That would be most kind," he said. "I'm Randol Cox and this is my brother, Jip."

"Deuc said this ship was made of metal, but I didn't believe it," Randol said walking over to one of the struts and rubbing his fingers on it. He rubbed his fingers together and rust-colored granules stuck to them. "And this is your blood."

"You told them everything," I said to Deuc.

"Iron blood and a mixture Professor Belo invented," Deuc said, ignoring me. "It's a preservative that protects against the sea spray."

Georgios led the Riptiders to the garden and the kitchen. Sometimes he seemed to be too kind and unconcerned with his own welfare. He did not put the welfare of those he knew best before the needs or wants of those he did not know intimately. This generosity of spirit, however, never seemed to harm him.

I hadn't paid much attention to Randol. Deuc had absorbed all my attention, but as we went upstairs to view our quarters on the second floor, I studied the pirate and was surprised to see a ratfin peek out from the band of his hat. In-fin hissed his surprise and the other ratfin hid in the folds of the hat and Randol's unbound brown curly hair. In Timbol's room, we showed them the schematics for the Seastead. Randol asked questions about everything, but when Merl offered to take them up to the masthead, he wasn't interested.

"We've seen enough of the ocean," Randol said.

Jip talked mostly to Desiree. I could hear him talking about Elathe and all the goods they had there. He stopped to touch everything: the new seedlings with their tender shoots, the solar panels, the equipment in the boiler room, the sensors, and, naturally, Desiree. He had a hand on her back, shoulder, or waist at every conceivable opportunity: whenever she laughed, which was often, or to help her up or down stairs.

She raised an eyebrow at me, so I knew she was well aware of the attentions, but then she didn't seem to mind.

I made sure to lead the way downstairs and turned off the UV lights. I hoped they wouldn't peer too carefully at the hydroponic pool. They were mostly interested in the vat of Iron Blood and the formula for the serum and then Merl took them over to the pumps and boiler schematics.

Now Randol had even more questions.

"How much blood does it take to coat the ship?"

"Five pints for 1,500 square feet."

I watched him make the calculation. He'd need each of us alive. We'd designed the Seastead to be sustainable for our small group.

Down here, Jip's fingers prying into everything made me the most nervous. It was only a matter of time until he triggered the opening. But he got bored in the dark, because Desiree hadn't joined us, I suspected. She'd begged off the rest of the tour to start dinner.

"Make tea," I'd told her, and she nodded. I didn't want her serving glasses of that suspiciously fresh water.

With the tour over, the Riptiders seemed to relax. There were some curiosities on board the Seastead, but no unpleasant surprises. We had no weapons. They'd kept their pistols holstered.

We sat in the kitchen and watched Desiree prepare the food. Georgios helped her chop tomatoes and kale. In-fin crawled down from around my neck and sniffed at Randol. His ratfin poked over the top of his hat and when he set it down the ratfin crawled up onto the table and squabbled with mine briefly. Then they began to play.

"Well, our ratfin are friendly," Randol said. They curled up together in the brim of his hat.

"Jip, get us some things from the ship to share with these folks," he said, the returned his attention to us. "So everyone wants to know about how we Riptiders built our island."

He began to relate the story of the Riptiders, which we all knew, but it was entertaining to hear it directly from a pirate. The Riptiders in this version were smart and resourceful, not greedy.

In the middle of the story, Jip returned with a jug of rum and some small cakes. I watched him watching Desiree and enjoying his food. His tongue loosened considerably with drink.

"Now what happened on La Merde?" he asked.

"General Balor," I said.

"Balor," Randol said. "He's a bastard. Doesn't give up either. He's troubled us more than once. We're not going to send our sons all over the seas after him though. Although we might not stop some of the younger ones from getting a mind to do just that. How many soldiers did he bring?"

He wanted information, but he had probably heard all this from Deuc and was just confirming the details.

After dinner, Merl, Desiree, Timbol, and Jip climbed into the tower. "Where's your juice?" Randol asked straight up.

But we didn't have any contraband: no drugs and our alcohol hadn't had time to ferment.

Randol sniffed at the kelp liquid Abrador had brought. "Why not?" he said and tipped the bottle back into his mouth.

I looked up and watched them watching us and wondered how much Merl was sharing with the inquisitive pirates. Deuc went out on the platform and began to play his guitar. The strumming swept over the sea.

I began to giggle. It was impossible to hide it in these close quarters from these attentive men. I used my old trick, thinking of the ratfin, but even this struck me as absurd. My body shook with laughter.

Randol turned on me. "What's so funny? Is it our hats?"

"No, ratfin," I said. "I've kept them as pets ever since I was little."

"Aye," he said. "I had them too as a lad. I used to use them for my experiments. I kept this one here, name's Darwin. He refused to die this one."

That sobered me at last. It sobered us all.

They asked us if we'd like to board their ship, Kyklopes. It looked to offer far more luxury. I was afraid that once there, however, the Riptiders would sail off with us. We'd already escaped captivity once and I wasn't ready to be imprisoned for my blood again. There was no way to escape that misfortune of birth. Still, I might have joined him. I was afraid of our rocky, unsteady Seastead with its metal clanking struts and tiny confined platform. How long would it last?

We stayed late into the night on the deck listening to Deuc's song and Randol's pirate escapades until he retired to his ship. Late into the night, I heard Desiree laughing. The next morning, I watched Jip stumble out of her room.

Later, he, Deuc, and Randol descended from the plank.

Randol strode out.

"Now show us what's under here," he said. He stomped on the deck. There was a hollow, clanging sound. "Come now. There's something," he shouted when we remained silent.

Timbol went down to the engine room and shortly after we heard the clunk and watched the surface of the platform split. I saw Deuc's surprise. He hadn't known. We could have kept it secret. But Desiree was holding her head. She'd drank and talked too much, and I looked over at Merl who looked equally hung over. Or, he had. Neena brought them out glasses of the cool water. We knew it quickly cleared a hangover.

"Might as well," she said.

Randol looked into the pool. He scanned it with his eyes.

"And you had visitors?" Randol asked.

He knew that too. Who had talked so much? I couldn't help but like Randol. He had a confident air, interesting stories, and a stout laugh. But I remembered his talk of experiments on the ratfin. There was much about him I did not know, but I knew the Riptiders did not reach out to help others as the waters rose. They had saved only their own. We Seasteaders had done the same, though. How many people were waiting in line for the ferry? Had I even looked for my own mother? What if she had somehow survived the landslide? Did it matter? We'd only ended up with a raft. How many more would have fit on the *mokol*? Not even one.

"One visitor, but yes, he said more will come," Georgios said. "Trainers. They want to teach us their ways and take us to see their place."

"What do they want from you?"

"We don't know."

"Find out," he said to Deuc. "Deuc will stay here. He wants to learn, too."

Deuc looked like he wanted to protest, but the Riptiders did not allow debate. They followed the ship captain's orders. "Of course," Deuc said.

The Riptide galleon sailed off and left a sullen Deuc behind.

"They don't consider you one of them, Deuc. You're not family so when it comes down to it you are dispensable," Georgios said.

"Yes, I know," Deuc said. "I don't need another of your lectures, Georgios. They want what they've always wanted from me, information. But they can be useful to us too. They helped build this place. They transported the metal out here. They already consider this part of their territory, but they're not going to lose life over it, unless there's something valuable. You're valuable, of course. But just as good here, out of the way, and less trouble, out of sight out of mind. The Riptiders won't fight over us out here. That source of fresh water, though..."

~ 12 ~

MULIAN TRAINING

The Mulians sent three trainers to our Seastead. Abrador was not among them. The trainers vaguely resembled our first emissary. They had discernible parts: mangled-looking heads, long robes, trunks and tentacles, soft upper bodies and encrusted lower torsos, usually mounted on a soft cephalopod foot.

The one who taught us language had a long, curved head like a seahorse with a bright green sheen. The agricultural instructor had slits in the side of his robes, in shades of blue, where tentacles stuck out at crablike angles, but were covered with suckers like an octopus. The swimming instructor looked the most human, in swirling shades from peach to black, with a long slender smooth body on two webbed feet. Adi often swam unrobed in silvery loops around the pool. Adi's enormous round head stuck out of the water giving us plenty of opportunity to marvel at its spikes, barnacles, and rows of eyes sparkling like jewels.

The Mulians used the pronoun Adi, which meant simply "one of us." The swimmer never gave me any sense of gender and I thought of the swimmer as Adi even in my head.

Merl, who never picked up even a little of the language, called the trainers Green Singer, Blue Farmer, and The Purple Frog.

The first time they said their names I could not hear them. They sounded like a hum, a mewl, and a croak. I realized that the name that Abrador gave us was not his true name, but one easier for us to understand.

While the trainers worked with us, they lived in a dome-shaped globe just a little smaller than our Seastead platform about 30 feet below the surface of the pool. They came onto the platform only while working with us and on special occasions. It was a hardship for them to spend too much time in our air. The corrosion seeped too quickly into their porous skins. At night, we could see their pale, green globe lit up, phosphorescent underwater and see their shadows moving beneath its semi-translucent surface. The water carried the sound of their voices humming and singing into the night. Occasionally, I thought I heard approximations of our names and sprinkled laughter.

It must have been amusing to teach us.

We began with language lessons and everyone on the Seastead, curious, took part. It began with humming, then singing, and only later the separation of words. Their language consisted of spoken words, song, and telepathy. Much of the sense of it came mind to mind. We had to become receptive first and we practiced humming, chanting, and meditation.

Merl quickly became frustrated. He couldn't discern the speech and never heard the Mulians in his head. He pretended at first and then finally admitted, "I don't hear a thing."

He retreated to his engineering projects. He wouldn't swim either, he was too afraid of the water, so his lessons ended there. Neena also struggled with the new sounds of words, but she liked the singing and swimming. Desiree got the language quite well, Georgios and Timbol passably. Deuc picked it up quickly with his musical sensibility.

"I like it better than our own," he said.

He was best at the speech and the inflection, but I surpassed him in understanding the telepathy.

I could hear the Mulians talking in my head almost from the beginning. It reminded me of the imaginary conversations I held with the Octavians as a child, but I missed some of the nuances of the spoken Mulian because I missed the music, or I tried to translate the Mulian words into my own tongue and missed the differences.

Deuc said he could not get the telepathy, but one day I felt him singing Mulian in my head. "I had a breakthrough," he said.

The language training went slowly. Meanwhile, I tried to get a better sense of Neena and Deuc's growing friendship. One night after dinner, I instigated a game of Cardinal with them.

"Sure, I'm too tired to do anything else," Deuc said.

We were all exhausted by trying to understand and form Mulian words and having the trainers in our heads.

It was fun to have new player in Cardinal to throw off the balance of my usual planning. I was too used to the patterns of the others' play. Deuc knew the game well. He played to win, but when he got bored he began to throw hands. Neena made moves for elegance, as if she had rules all her own, playing for the rhythm of the game, without a thought for winning. She approached everything that way, making beauty and rhythms appear where there were none. They both saw the world in interesting, but completely different, ways from me. Whereas Georgios and I saw the world, as far as I could tell, exactly the same. Timbol and I were in a great deal of agreement, but there were things that interested him that I was not as interested in, details and marine life, whereas I focused often on the future and plans. Desiree and Merl were freer people less serious, more focused on their particular pleasures. Desiree loved cooking and craftwork and Merl loved tinkering and concoctions.

Neena and Deuc composed songs together. He played and she added her poetry as lyrics. They sang together. More often than not, she would grow silent.

"I love to hear my words in his voice," she said. "They sound so beautiful. It is as if I had not written them."

They were becoming good, if unlikely, friends.

Eventually the Mulians could communicate well enough with us that we could begin our swimming lessons. Already they had taken us into the water each day as part of our language lessons and we had learned to paddle across the surface. Georgios, Timbol, Deuc and I and even Neena made progress. Merl refused to have anything to do with it and Desiree managed to become buoyant, but not much more. She was beautiful in the sunlit water though with her dark hair shiny and sleek as a seal. I watched Georgios watching her.

Before we could dive, we had to apply an algae-scented lotion to our faces every morning and night for a week to prepare the skin. We entered the water in the outdoor training pool, up to our chests and they brought up a basket filled with an assortment of purple, light blue, and pale green pearlescent tentacles. They were beautiful laying still in the basket woven of sea stuffs. But they felt strange: firm and tumescent yet spongy and pliable. It stung when the trainers affixed them to our faces three on each side down our cheekbones, two along each side of the nose and three shorter ones over our top lips. These were to help with breathing, but also to cover the nose and mouth, which were culturally erotic. They tickled, but wearing them, the water felt safer. To get us used to the depths and make it easier to breathe, we had to apply the tentacles. The weird sensations disappeared when we went underwater. I caught on to it quite quickly and was praised as a good swimmer.

Once we learned to swim, our agricultural lessons began. We swam down to the kelp beds below the trainers' dome. In Mulian society everyone grows their own food.

"So, they expect us to go there? Underwater. To live?" asked Georgios.

"For as long as it takes to learn their ways," I said. "They can teach us how to save ourselves. They will show us. Besides, aren't you curious?"

"Of course, but this is enough of an adventure for me. I can't see myself underwater."

"I can," I said. "See myself underwater. Maybe I always have seen myself in hazy ripples."

He was silent. We had an inkling then of what was ahead for us.

When the lesson was over, we each detached our tentacles and placed them in small separate baskets labeled with our names. These were our tentacles now. The trainers showed us how to sprinkle our tentacles with small gold flakes, a kind of food that keeps them healthy in some way (I still found it difficult to understand our trainers' thick accents and muffled voices). I could mostly understand their ideas.

We all, except Merl who refused to take part, had deep purple sucker marks across our faces where the tentacles had been, and they gave us a glittery blue green gel to help our skin heal and to help the suckers stick better to our faces next time. I was afraid it would permanently change the quality of my skin. Maybe for the better? Softer? Now it seems a funny fear.

The lotion I applied every day to my face did begin to change the texture of my skin. It became softer and smoother, but also tougher and rubbery. One day, I realized that the tiny flakes of gold in the sparkly gel we applied to our faces was similar to the glittery "tentacle food". We were teaching them to feed off our faces.

Our skin became soft and stretchy, but after long periods of diving and being underwater in tentacles, when we pulled them off the places where the tentacles had clung began to ache and itch. Patches of skin on my face sloughed off. We had no mirrors, but I could see how it looked on the others, like a rash of pox.

They continued language and culture training, teaching us more complicated songs and rituals.

Adi told me, "Until you are able to change, you will not be able to attain your Octavia. You will always fall short of what you've envisioned."

They ought to have known. This was why the Mulians had gone underwater long ago.

They'd taken the word Octavia from me. They used it for their meaning, utopia. They'd learned the idea from me.

Toward the end of our Mulian training, the Riptiders returned.

~ 13 ~

JUMPING OFF

The Riptiders made Deuc go to Mu to maintain his loyalty to them. They wanted most of us to stay above water on the Seastead to donate blood and I wondered how long the Seastead would be able to stay afloat without us.

Neena, Deuc, and I would go. Timbol, Desiree, Merl, and Georgios would stay.

I wondered at our decision to send Neena to Mu. Was her life worth less because she was an artist? But it came down to her choice, and she wanted to go to Mu. The Mulians tempted us by saying they had something down there to save us, to turn back the corrosion and purify the sea. We each had our own reasons for wanting to make the journey. Neena wanted to write poems about them and to follow the path she felt Professor Alexandra had set for her. Deuc sought to bring back secrets to the Riptiders and, also, he felt most at home adventuring amongst the fringe.

I wanted to find utopian secrets and visit the imagined city of my childhood dreams, but I didn't want to leave Georgios. My two conflicting desperate desires competed. I felt sanded by them, polished, vibrant, and ready to descend into the sea. I remembered the pain, the fear of being separated from Georgios when we were leaving La Merde and I went to find Neena. That separation was only hours. After we reunited it all seemed bearable--together--even though we were casting out onto an uncertain ocean and there was the threat of drowning, of rusting, and of being eaten by sharks.

Before we went, we drained as much blood as we could to help the Seastead, although we were already blood light. We were lightheaded and dizzy. Perhaps if we'd been at full blood, the whole departure would have seemed less surreal. Maybe we would have had the sense to stay.

The Mulians arranged a special time for our departure. Our arrival in Mu would be in their season of *sivan* coinciding with their hydrophoria festival, an auspicious time. There was a full moon on the eve of our departure and Neena, Deuc, and I had tried to busy ourselves all day. Even so, we were perched on the edge of the pool too early. We had our things beside us in rubber packs. They were not many. We had few possessions to begin with on the islands, even fewer on the Seastead and our trainers had told us they would take us to get the things we would need to live when we arrived. When we'd asked them what to bring, they had said, "Nothing."

Still, Neena had to take her journals and her pens and Deuc his lute. I wanted one of everything I thought the others would have brought, I took a map from Timbol and seeds and spices from Desiree. I pondered for a while what Merl would bring and considered batteries, serum, and electrodes and finally brought a small solar panel--more as a symbol than for practical use. For Merl, preparation meant making do with what you had and using your brain to capacity. I figured he would trust to have the materials to innovate once he arrived. Georgios made me take a deck of Cardinal cards. They turned out to be a prized possession. I wanted to have a bit of each of my tribe with me for comfort. It was, I would learn, a very Mulian approach.

We waited beside the pool until the bubbling began in the center of it where the moon shone through and the spikes of Mulian crowns broke through the surface. They were lavender lengths tipped with pink pearls that glowed silver in the moonlight. I looked back at Georgios hovering on the platform behind me. He'd been making himself look busy, touching ropes and nets, or some such.

"They're below," I said. "I'm going."

He nodded. He didn't say, "You don't have to do this."

He knew I did.

"Wait," he said. "I've one more thing for you."

He slipped a coin into my hand.

"They are not the only ones that can leave you tokens."

It was a medallion he'd carved of precious wood. The picture on it was of a cypress tree. I strung it around my neck.

I gave Georgios In-fin. I unhooked the sweet creature from his place around my neck.

"Look after my ratfin," I said, handing the ratfin over. In-fin quickly crawled up Georgios' arm and curled around his neck sniffing at his ear.

"I will." Georgios said.

As I said goodbye to Georgios, I watched him watching Desiree. If I was gone long, their relationship was inevitable. I was sending them into each other's arms, but I could see no way around it. He had to work on his project here and pacify the Riptiders. I needed to go to find out about the Mulians and what lay beneath us--the key to our destiny and our opportunity to, as I had always envisioned, become one with the water. We needed to learn first and see if this was something we could accept and nurture in our world. It was foolish to think that we could sustain a love apart in those tumultuous times and at such a distance between surface and sea, but I could not turn down the opportunity to go live among the Mulians. I had to know what was below.

The moment before I jumped into the pool though, I wanted nothing but to stay on the Seastead alone with Georgios. I wanted that more than anything to be beside Georgios forever, just sitting, and holding hands.

It was almost enough for me. Almost. I remembered my promise to my grandmother, "Don't you leave him. When you love, you stay." I would break that promise because there were things I wanted more. I yearned to see the Mulian city, and I longed to create a social structure and a peaceful place. I wanted, in some way, to defeat the soldiers who destroyed my grandmother's house. It was a residual of my deep longing to step in between my father and my mother's arguments. Not to raise my fist to father, but to gaze at him and, with one look, take all the fight and anger out of him. How that rage had infected him in the first place was a mystery. I wanted to dissolve his anger so that he could float forever in love and lap at my mother's feet proffering only kisses, as she deserved.

If I had not wanted this more, then I could have stayed with Georgios. It may have been enough.

I could have given up my savior dreams, but even if I could have, I could not have been certain of Georgios and myself. There was the way he looked at Desiree. There was the way I still looked at Deuc. We did not know that our life together could be counted on, certainly not enough to risk the fate of the world, certainly not considering the world and its risks. I had no choice, being myself in that moment, but to descend. Looking back from an age, I never would have gone, but then I would not be this person I am now had I not gone to Mu. There is no way to change the decision. *Praise water!*

The Mulians pointed to the tentacles. I applied them for the last time. I would never take them off again. The places on my face where I chose to put them were where they would always be. I affixed two on the sides of my nose and one on my temple to drape down and cover my nostrils. All of these were blue. I placed a row of smaller lavender tentacles cross my upper jaw line to veil my erotic mouth and stuck two larger purple-green ones into my dimples. Neena decorated her face with light blue and turquoise tentacles and applied more than she needed. She was not afraid to become other. Either that or she wanted to be very sure to breathe. Deuc picked deep blue and black tentacles and used just a few large ones. The fact that his lips were hidden made me want to see them even more. I was beginning to find the tentacles appealing. One day I would enjoy the touch of them.

Because we were diving down so far, we wore the helmets as well. Deuc, Neena and I put on our helmets on over our heads. I felt the suckers attach themselves to my bare skin, the uncovered places on my cheeks, behind my ears, the back of my neck, my throat. The sensations were more familiar, but still odd. The shell material before my eyes tinted everything a pale green.

In my head, I was already composing letters to Georgios, and thinking of what I would say to him when I returned.

"I am sliding into the water," I said.

In my head, when I talked to Georgios, I felt like I was lying. Everything would sound adventurous, ethereal, lovely, and passionate. It was not a lie, but how could I be passionate without him? When I was with the Mulians, I felt every moment deeply. Every moment felt like my last. I held close my passion for Georgios.

Once I was tentacled, for the first 20 or so feet it was just like diving in the ocean, and then it was like diving down into the deepest, darkest ocean, but then ahead of me the water became lighter, and we entered a tunnel and it seemed to be flowing down. It grew lighter and lighter in the tunnel. It had occurred to me more than once on the platform that I did not particularly like fish or the ocean. I liked it from above, seeing it as part of the setting, but I did not like plunging into it. I did not like the three dimensionality of it, not knowing what was beneath me. I did not like the kind of polluted saltiness of it: salt that tasted of algae and tuna. I did not like the little fish that darted against my skin or the larger mammoth shapes I imagined rising beneath and beside me. The ocean sunk fear into me. Its terrors struck deep into my subconscious. Still, I went without a struggle.

Past the deep cold part of the water, it opened into a pale blue dawn. We drifted on a current past dunes and dunes of soft brown and in pockets bright white. I heard a ringing across the dunes sometimes louder, sometimes softer like ambient bells or cooing mourning doves. The further we went, the fewer and further between the white patches became and it was like an underwater desert of rolling sand. Soon, I noticed that we were traveling slowly. There was barely any current at all.

Even though I was better at telepathy than any other Seasteader, I struggled with the Mulian mind-to-mind talk. Underwater it was essential. There was no other way to communicate and the deeper we went as we traveled down, the easier it became.

I heard the Mulian voices in my head. I heard the whale song. I heard their trumpets and their bells.

I looked at Neena and Deuc. We had traveled even farther down than I had expected. After a while Adi swam to the side. We swam the rest of the way. It was warm and stagnant outside the current. Deuc swam in the strange upright way we had practiced.

"Praise mountaintop!" I thought, then corrected myself, "Praise water!" I had no difficulty breathing and the pressure of the depths did not crush me. I was safe in the Mulian currents.

I struggled to swim correctly and wondered what all my plans and ideals would come to when I didn't even know how to move. Gradually, we floated into a horizontal, upright position.

There was a current, but it flowed across what I would have thought was the ocean floor. The water was warm, but it grew colder. Sinking, I felt alone for the first time ever in my life, alone no possibility of love ahead of me, nothing left to long for. Never had Georgios felt so far away, so lost from every possibility of return. Gone. Gone. Forever. I sank with Deuc and Neena beside me and our bodies were cold, our faces foreign and tentacled. I imagined I would never again be warm.

We followed the spiked headdress ahead of us. Down. In the dark, they looked like pieces of ebony coral. Coal-colored crowns. I could barely see anything. It had been night above.

As the Mulians, Neena, Deuc and I traveled down, a pathway opened ahead, a lighter shade of blue streaking through the deeper blue beside it. The water grew warm inside the pathway. When I reached my hand outside, it was quickly chilled. Then, I could see topography below. Nothing appeared distinct, as I gazed through the moving water, but I saw round shapes, hills and valleys, roads, and a round bubble cluster surrounded by lights.

In front of me, the bubbles that moved through my hands were shiny and round. They sparkled as they accelerated towards me. Here, I lost track of my orientation, and I would not regain it. It was no longer possible to think of the direction of where I was headed as down or the place where I had come from as up. Where I had been oriented head down in a diving position, I was now moving forward as if walking. I felt pushed forward by the warm water. I could see the city. Its towers and domes were shaded, deeply etched before the backdrop of the ocean so that the whole city looked distinct and deep. It would be a long time before I saw the city from that perspective again, from the height and distance of arrival.

From above, this was how Mu looked. In the center of Mu was a golden pyramid and at the top of the pyramid was a golden sun. Extending out over the pyramid was a translucent, billowing, green membrane. The entire civilization was encased within a sack like a jellyfish. How the sun was there underwater able to be looked at directly I could not fathom. I stared and stared at it. There was warmth, but it did not burn.

Looking at Mu, I thought it was entirely possible that I would never return to the surface. How could I see this alien city and then return to my other life? That moment, when it would have been most easy, or at least possible, to go back to the Seastead, was the one moment when I was not considering it. Later, when it would have been difficult or impossible, the idea of return to Georgios and air consumed me.

Four roads in each direction extended from the pyramid. There were four towers at the ends of the roads. Each of the four sectors was a pale color: lavender, periwinkle, aqua, and green. I learned later they were colored by the foods grown upon the different soils and that the Mulians rotated the crops each year. There was a white coliseum embedded on the rise of an open, green park apart from the pyramid. Below the park, I recognized the raised beds we had learned to make to grow our food. Then the sides sloped down into darkness. Mulians lived in warren-like caves that extended beneath the surface city.

The faces of my companions were unreadable underneath their helmets. To me, in the darkness of our approach, they appeared as blobs of strange matter. But I sensed a well of emotion in Neena. She hovered above the view, swimming slowly, taking it all in. I knew she was affected. Deuc continued his movement, and I sensed his fear. This was more than we expected. He'd made a huge sacrifice to gain the political goodwill of the pirates.

We entered the city through an arch of whale bone.

"This is not our entire empire. This is the city Mu," Abrador said.

I saw masses of pink pearl crowns and wavy pillar bodies and heard a reverberating hum. The Mulians were lined up to greet us. I was elated and exhausted as soon as I saw them. How will we communicate, I worried.

I could not understand the first Mulian who approached me. It was not like language training when words were spoken often in regular and predictable patterns. Later, I learned that the Mulians were just saying standard greetings and well wishes for the hydrophoria holiday. The proper response was just to repeat the words back, but our trainers did not teach us this, so we struggled to understand and quickly became tired, frustrated, and overwhelmed.

There was a ceremony and celebration that was mostly a crowd of strange rubbery bodies, foul offerings of salty and seaweedy food and drinks, and a long reverberating hum of noise that pounded at my head and made my tentacles bounce against my face and tap at my lips and nose in an unpleasant dance. Then we were guided into a domed building.

It sparkled white and light turquoise but was overlaid by a deep blue and black pattern, a mosaic design. Beneath the dome, we were led down a dark corridor. We had entered a cave. It was dark, but shimmering reflections of water and light danced on the coral lining around us.

I felt muffled, sleepy. A Mulian trainer, I think it was The Blue Farmer, took my hand in his rubbery mitt and led me forward. How far had we traveled? How far had we come? How many times had my arms pushed aside the water, stroking into the waves? I knew that the sea beneath the Seastead was many fathoms, but I'd never dove down more than thirty myself.

The Singer led Deuc away down a corridor and The Farmer led Neena and I down another.

Neena and I would room together.

When she took off her helmet, I saw her tears and knew she had been deeply affected by our descent. Something about the air and the pressure change made us sleepy and compliant. I was led into a dark room, and I sunk down into a soft surface that surrounded me with a feeling of peace and tranquility. I could not easily sleep for the dancing reflections on the surfaces around me. On the ceiling? On the floor? I watched for a long time torn between watching the patterns and falling asleep until strangely it occurred to me that my eyes had long been closed, but I could still see the patterns, tentacles, reflections of waves and light undulating across the ceiling, distinctly moving behind my eyelids. I became annoyed tossing in the bedding, which felt like it was made of the softest sand, but still loose and gritty. I wanted only the silence, calm, and peace inside my own head. I wanted only to sleep. Suddenly, the light and movement stopped. At last, I slept.

I awoke in a small room with slick wet walls and soft blue gleam under a blue light. It was like a dream of death. I felt glued to the bed I was in--a shell shape, half buried in its sandy covering and moved by waves. I had vague hallucinations and felt a tickling along my chin. I put my hands to my mouth and whiskered tendrils suctioned against my fingertips. I pulled them aside in horror and fascination. These were my tentacles. On my face. I slept again. When I woke up the soft tendrils were still there. My lips and mouth, once thin and wrinkled, felt full and wrinkled instead.

A smooth headed Mulian appeared in the doorway and then at my bedside. Adi (again the Mulian pronoun seemed most appropriate) had small tendrils around their mouth. It looked like a soft pink mustache. One day, I would kiss a tentacled mouth like this and discover a new sensation.

Adi poured a hot liquid into a small, ornate silver cup. Its rim was etched with Mulian swimmers. The drink was salty and spicy. I recognized it as the kelp-green liquid Abrador had given us on the Seastead. The liquid was intoxicating. *Mélange*, the Mulians called it.

Neena rose from another shell bed in the room and we both felt rejuvenated after drinking the mélange. It removed the pressure and fuzz from our minds.

When the Mulian left us, we began to explore. We walked out of the dark sleeping room and followed the light down the open hall. We did not dare open any doors, but at the end of our compartment was a cave with pool in its center lined by smooth green stones. There was a porthole in the wall of the cave looking out to the ocean. The water within the pool bubbled and frothed and a sweet scent rose from it.

Neena and I slipped off our clothes and into the water. I let it bubble up around my face. The water I was sitting in did not appear to have a floor just a seat and stones, but in the middle, there was just a darkening of the blue and it may have gone down further, how far I did not know.

"What did you think when you saw the city?" I asked Neena.

"It made me want to write," Neena said. "Alexandra was right. If she led me here, she was right to do so. I only wish she could have seen it."

As we sat in the tub, a small grey eye appeared at the porthole. The eye was surrounded by a deep grey. A humpbacked whale peered in at us. She frequented these depths. I was reminded again of how far underwater I had come as if an enormous creature had swallowed me.

Part Three: Mu

~ 14 ~

IN MU

In the morning, our language trainer Green Singer arrived. I was glad to see her, but she would not say more than a few words in our language. We were to speak only Mulian now. She brought us our first Mulian robes. They were long rubbery capes that fell below our feet and trailed behind us. They would protect us from the cold sea and cover our strange looking bodies. Cloaked in the rubbery draping we looked almost Mulian. Neena wore pink. My robe was deep purple. Deuc's was nearly black.

For many of the Mulians, the capes hid their soft mollusk feet. When I'd first seen the crowd of robed Mulians, I'd thought the robes were identical, but up close I could see the difference between them, Neena's robe had swirling patterns, mine looked like waves, and Deuc's looked like the night sky. Neena immediately put her robe on over her nakedness, and I don't think she wore any other clothes again for the rest of the time we were there.

"It's so *vahoma,*" she said, remembering the Mulian word for soft, a combination of breath--va--and water--homa.

The robe was soft and pliable but held its form. It felt like the same texture as the coins I had received, but thinner. It was, like all objects in Mu, a living thing with its own will.

Neena and I, testing the language with a small vocabulary and some discomfort, always spoke in short, simple sentences now. It had the effect of making us sound earnest and sage.

Long, winding complicated sentences like General Balor's speeches only had the effect of making him sound disconnected. I tried to remember this lesson, but I also found I soon began to miss being able to use unusual words and have long conversations. I missed the ease of understanding.

Soft was not quite the right word for the robes. Now we used the nearest word, one with the essence of the meaning we wanted. These simplifications made us sound quaint.

The robes were sleek against the skin. The underside of the robe was a little wet and malleable so that it was like wearing a coating of lotion. Our skin grew soft. Georgios, how I wanted to touch you with my newly soft skin. I did not want to return, however; I wanted to bring you to me. I could have asked for it. Maybe it could have been done, but it seemed the decision had been made. I had to explore Mu and you had to map the ocean.

I was not comfortable unclothed, and I always wore a short shift underneath my Mulian robe. Deuc hated the robes and would only wear them for formal Mulian gatherings, but usually he was shirtless with jeans on in a makeshift half robe he invented and wore like a kilt. The Mulians found his display of his under body scandalous. Because of this, some of the younger ones began to adopt Deuc's style. I wondered if the Mulians ever regretted our intrusion.

"It's hell to work in these things," Deuc said, although we were given separate gardening robes, which were shorter and rougher on the outside and of a paler color that matched the kelp-green crops. These robes were specially made after the harvest celebration and blessed to sow bountiful crops. Deuc only reliably wore his robe in the cooler months.

Once we were dressed, the trainer took us to get the things we needed to live in Mu and to show us to our gardens, which were told to plant immediately. Every Mulian grew their own food, and we would not be accepted into this community if we could not.

The quantity of things the Mulians deemed we needed astounded me. In addition to our gardening tools and supplies, they included a bronze tea service on a platter, an incense burner, a collection of vases, a broom, and various sizes of ornately decorated bottles filled with spices and salts. I had never had so many objects in my life and could not discern for the life of me why all of these were needed for a short stay in Mu. I grew suspicious and wary. My trainer went to one of the large dark caves and retrieved these collections for us. I imagined they came from a large storeroom. I was right about this. However, there were no manufacturers. Instead, the workers in the storerooms looked after the objects, cleaning, polishing, and mending any object that had lost their previous caretakers and finding the best new homes for them. In fact, these items had been made long ago, and we were receiving sets that had been used by ancestors who had moved on. The sets Neena and I received were similar but different. Hers was pink and blue. Mine was red and bronze.

Objects and caring for objects was a large part of Mulian culture. It was part of their purpose to care for what they had. The objects were treated like living beings with souls. We were expected to spend time each day polishing the items, to keep them in their proper places, and to use them with reverence and respect. There were punishments for losing or harming things.

Our cache of objects included our gardening tools: bronze trowels, a bucket, and a shovel with a bronze handle. These implements were retrieved from a storeroom, but then kept in the greenhouse. We were assigned chests there in which to keep our work robes and gardening tools.

"Later, I will take you to retrieve your seeds," The Blue Farmer said, in a reverent tone. "First, you must be received by the community. Return now to your home and I will come for you at sundown."

Neena and I looked at each other. Of course, we had not been paying attention and could not tell exactly where we were. After some time, it became easy to find our way. The city was arranged in quadrants. By observing the light and color, you could find your way. Although, the colors shifted quadrants with the seasons. When we arrived, our cave was located in the south end of the blue quadrant.

Neena and I often sat and talked in the bubbling pool within our cave to process new events and prepare ourselves for the next encounter. Once we had our objects, our next initiation into Mu was to meet the Mulian council.

We put on our robes. The hardest part was arranging our hair. The Mulians, of course, did not have hair. There were no brushes or gels to contain locks and wisps, but they did have clasps for the robes and to restrain their tendrils; so, we used those. Not long after we arrived, Neena found the tools to shave her head. Her hair, after that, grew in slowly, fine and pale green. We decided it was a result of living in the *homa* of Mu--the light, breathable liquid that the Mu lived in--faintly sweet and not salty. The homa also had a soft scent to it that changed with the seasons. At hydrophoria, in the summer, it was permeated by a damp lavender scent.

I was reluctant to give up my hair and taking note of what happened to Neena's head made me more so, although her shaven look did, along with her robes, give her an elegant and youthful appearance. Instead, I kept my hair and let it grow and tangle within my tentacles. By the end of my time in Mu, I had long dreadlocks that began to look like sleek tentacles and then chains of barnacles as those attached to us, a sign of respect and our Mulian integration. By then, many aspects of my appearance had changed.

Green Singer came to lead us to the council. We stopped and got Deuc from the lavender sector. I was relieved to see he was wearing his robe and had his long hair pinned back with a shell.

We walked past the living stones underground and up a ramp to the lawn around the coliseum. It had low walls and a sunken center. There were bells chiming and a large group of Mulians--in all their sizes, blue, green, and lavender shades, and sea-creature shapes--assembled on the open lawn before the coliseum. This was our first Mulian concert. Green Singer took us out among the Mu. They surrounded us on their pale blue-green field, standing on a hillock with their concert encircling us.

From my early days in Mu, what I remember most is music. My hearing was impaired when I first got there. My ears felt constantly plugged and the pressure would not relieve. It wasn't until I'd been there six months that I noticed one day while harvesting kelp that I could hear with crispness that I'd been lacking, and I cried with joy and relief. The Mulians farming nearby wondered at this strangeness. They, who did not cry, came and tasted my tears with their tentacles, which made me cry harder at my alienation, at being surrounded by odd creatures, at being separated from my loved ones. I think the event earned me some respect though among the Mu. I, with my ability to create sea-tears, became in their minds more of a sea creature after that. It was one of many times I was overwhelmed by my experience in Mu.

However, when they first brought me to the park to hear their strange instruments, sound still had that flat, muffled quality that reminded me of having earplugs in and of being underwater. It felt remote. They sang us welcome.

I looked at Deuc in his long, strange robe and thought of him shirtless on stage at Merops with his deep underwater voice layered beneath the electronics.

"I wanted to be taken seriously," he told me later, explaining why he had dressed in the Mulian style at that time and rarely after. "Now, I don't care. Clothes are tools, not art. They either keep us at the right temperature, protect us, or help us tell a story."

In Mu, there was no stage with a band of performers around it, however. Everyone performed. We were all part of the music. There was no celebrity. We worshipped each other. The concert took place in an open space with more light reflected from the water above the dome, casting waves of light down upon us. Mulians sang and, I later noticed, added sounds with tiny instruments of clacking shells, beads upon their garments and metal clasps. I did not notice these details at my first Mulian concert. I stared up at the dome and looked at the strange beings around me uncertainly. A heavenly music emanated without a clear source. It was beautiful and disorienting and it went on and on. As it did so my anxiety grew. The music was no longer beautiful, but a menace. I did not know when it would stop. I did not know when I would have a chance, to eat, to drink, to rest, to be alone as I so often needed to be in my early days in Mu. Later, when I acclimated, I could stay for hours at these concerts and participate. The first time, however, I was lost without time or perception of the culture. It was torturous in a way that now I cannot fathom. I do not even understand myself how I could have hated it so much then and loved it so much later. How we can change in ways unfathomable to ourselves. Praise water!

Light emanated from the music. There was light when the Mulians spoke. When they whispered in the dark, they betrayed themselves with light. We topsiders (as the Mulians called those who lived above the ocean) were the only ones who could hide in the dark. The Mulians were a community. We were outside of it, but only because of our lack of understanding.

Beside me, Deuc and Neena were also uncomfortable. When the Mulians finally finished with their welcome song, we topsiders were exhausted. Abrador lead us onto a hill to meet the Mulian Council.

The Council of Thirty-Three stood in a circle, covered in barnacles and tentacles, their faces indistinguishable to us that first time. They spoke, as one, in unison. We felt them speak.

"We know your people are on the brink. The waters have turned against them, and they have turned against each other. We know what this is like, to face extinction and to be afraid. We think we can help by offering a learning."

"Yes, that's why we are here," I said.

"It will take time," Abrador said.

"How long?" Deuc asked.

"Two years," said Abrador.

"No," I said.

"No," Deuc said. "You never told us our visit would be so long."

"But you knew this," Abrador said to me, and I realized that I had known in a way. I had said goodbye as if I'd known and if I hadn't imagined it Georgios had known our separation would last years, too.

"There are only 200 Mulians remaining," the council spoke into us again. "We have only the minimum to repopulate the world, a small number easily hidden, but ready to repopulate the world should humankind fail. But we would rather not take to the surface again. We are content here. We would rather you succeed, and we stay beneath the ocean."

"It will take time," Abrador repeated.

I knew in my heart that I had understood this all along, but I thought anxiously: They've taken me prisoner. Until I can speak their language, it is not safe for me to be free. I can never leave until I pass this test. I don't know if I can ever learn the language. They speak mind to mind. What if I cannot learn? They speak in bubbles, pockets of air. They speak in sounds like waves, so long underwater; all the tones are hushed, except for the deep, grunting breaths of air. I can hardly hear. How can I understand them?

They wanted us to learn their ways. They wanted to help our species, but we had to know them to do so.

I watched Deuc watching everything, calculating what we could take back to the Riptiders once the time--two years--had passed. Would it be worthwhile?

"The flutes," Abrador said, he meant the column of freshwater we'd swum down from the surface to the deep dark sea and finally the homa domes of Mu . "They don't last forever. We can't make them at a whim. We must work now. The flute will go and then, in two years' time or so, it will return."

"You are going to send us back?" I asked. I wanted to extract a promise, but Abrador turned from me.

For the first time, it occurred to me that I could die down here in this foreign land of Mu.

"Can I send word back?" I asked. "To Georgios."

"There is no way to send words, but we can send song," Abrador said.

I would learn, as soon as possible how to sing in Mulian. I would send back songs so Georgios would know I would be longer than we had thought, but that I would return.

When we had agreed to stay, I took Deuc aside.

"If I die here, Deuc," I said. "You make sure they send my body home. Promise. I want to know I will return to the air and land."

I told it to Neena too, but she seemed unconcerned. She was comfortable here. For this, I trusted Deuc. He understood my attachment to the Earth above.

While I remained in Mu there were many things I missed: foods, smells, textures, tastes. It wasn't only Georgios. But when I look back at my time in Mu, it seems I thought only of Georgios and that everything I did was so that I could return to him.

~ 15 ~

MULIAN LOVE

I could not rest until I learned Mulian song, sang it to the messenger, and knew that my thoughts had been carried to Georgios.

Fortunately, the messenger was close by. She was Varuna the Whale whose eye had greeted us that first day and who frequently lingered outside our quarters. I knew Varuna from the Seastead as well. She had surfaced there in the flute of clear water out of reach of the rust sea and the rust sharks. When I grew skilled enough, I could sing directly to Varuna mind to mind, but in those early days in Mu I was anxious. I needed to be sure of some tie to Georgios, some way to communicate with him.

We were told not to leave Mu proper, but I have never been obedient. I have always had my secret getaways: the marsh, my room, the market, Merops. I must have space to get away where my mind can roam free with its plans. Mu had many crevices, but none had that forbidden feel which drives me. The Mulians told me I could not go outside and so that was where I wanted to go. I had many havens in Mu. I loved to spend time in the wet gardens. I loved the temple and the lawn outside the coliseum. Perhaps, I wanted to swim in the sea outside the safety of the Mulian *homa*, because I spent so much time looking up into the lavender rimmed inky eye of Varuna the Whale. There looked to be wisdom in the deep blue ridges of her face.

When I felt sure and Green Singer agreed, that my song could be sung well enough for Varuna to translate, I put on the helmet again and slipped down through the water pool portal in my room out of the sweet homa and into the salty sea of the deepest ocean. My body felt free my limbs flowing behind me like the tentacles of a jellyfish. Varuna, who loomed so large outside of my translucent roof, was now further away than I had expected. She swam in the depths outside, encircling the core of Mu and I had to swim through the open translucent space. I pressed my hands against the field and slowly entered the murk. I was deep below, and I felt the pressure around me, as I had not before in Mu. It was not unbearable, but the salt of the sea felt rough after the softness of the homa. I was becoming more Mulian already than I realized. I swam to the whale and lashed tails and fins brushed my bare skin in the dark. Still, I felt relaxed and at ease, as always when I went away on my own. I went out to the whale, and I touched her ridges. She was large but welcoming. A fin spun the wrong way in my direction could end me, but I felt safe beside her bulk.

I called to Varuna. I felt we understood each other, both of us at peace in the deep sea. I did not have to struggle to communicate, to grow food, or worry I would offend her. I went close to her, and I sang to her of my longing. I hoped Georgios would understand enough Mulian to know that I would be away for longer than I had expected but that I loved him more than ever and would return. Would he understand that from the thrumming of a strange whale appearing alongside the Seastead? It seemed unlikely, but Varuna's clear eye reassured me.

I continued to go outside into the sea and sing my messages directly to Varuna. The more I went outside though the more aware I became of the dangers. It seemed worth the risk to get away. I knew of the electric eels, the sharp teeth in the dark, the lashes of leathery, ridged flails with poisonous darts. There were also currents that could change and make it difficult to return through the barrier. I knew of these dangers, and I came back sometimes with poisons in my system, bites, or electric scars. Usually, Varuna protected me.

Abrador warned me of other dangers.

"You should not venture out," he said.

I was not aware he had known of my travels. He could tell I was not dissuaded.

"At least do not go without a companion from Mu," he said. "There are other tribes of peoples, other Mulian enclaves. They will drain your iron blood and use it as medicine. They do not care about you."

Of course, this caught my attention and made me wary and fearful, but it did not stop me. I could not take another Mulian with me always; this would defeat my need for isolation. The longer I stayed in Mu, the more cautious I became and the less frequently I ventured out. As it grew colder below and the lavender and sun scent faded, I could commune with Varuna directly while sitting in the pool in my room and staring out at her big eye. I no longer needed to go out and I would not risk it.

Munan. It was in those first months that I learned the Mulian word for lover. *Munan.*

The Mulians intrigued me, but I did not see them as partners. My thoughts were too much with the surface, with all the plans for how we might survive the rising Rust Sea. It was entirely possible, I often felt, for me to overcome the differences between our bodies. There was always something sensual about them. They were made up of so many textures and unusual ridges and lumps. However, I could not bridge the gaps between our minds. I thought I needed that connection to the sky, the wind, the trees, and the flowers: surface world things. I sang songs to Georgios every day and sent them to him via Varuna the humpback whale, but at night I began to talk to Deuc.

"I'm learning about the music," he said.

He talked endlessly about the new rhythms and harmonies he was learning and what they meant. We wore the long robes with nothing underneath. I thought about Deuc's "nothing underneath" more than I wanted to. Often.

We grew close. I didn't notice that he never talked about himself: his family or friends. He never asked about me. I noticed this but didn't much care. In Mu, all my plans seemed far away and on hold.

Our encounters began in a chaste fashion, stroking hands and exchanging soft kisses. I did not imagine this tenderness had been his style at Merops. I did not think of Georgios or feel guilty about in these moments. I was lonely and I felt this touch was necessary to my peace of mind, my sanity. I envied Deuc's easy way among the Mulians and how he kept to his own habits and made new ones. Whereas I felt the Mulians were dragging myself underwater, forever. I was subsumed by their ways. At times, working in the garden, learning their crafts, I gave in and let go. At other times, when I could not find Varuna the Whale to send my songs to Georgios, I resisted. With Deuc, singing music from the surface and doing things of which the Mulians would have disapproved, I rebelled. In my heart, I knew, I could not be as I once was. I clung to Deuc as if he were shore. He was essential to my transition.

We were so different, Deuc and I. He was more moved by the arts and had a carefree attitude whereas I was interested in structure and wanted to plan each move. He was fiercely independent, quiet in an insular way I sought to penetrate, but could not. He was more often silent. I wanted to speak about everything. I missed Georgios, who loved to talk through ideas, too. Yet, I was adaptable in Mu. It was necessary. We each saw our way as an asset and the other's way as weakness. However, when Deuc and I were together, I began to have fantasies that I could become more like him, that I could be a partner to him and adopt his ways and be well. We would have fun together.

I have always been like this. I want to live out many lives. I see the threads of each of them. I am ready to join any one at any point. I saw this one life held out to me and, of course, I wanted to pick it up. In many ways, I wish I were a ratfin. Their lives are short so they may rapidly move on to the next life and see what awaits. I missed In-fin, who I had left with Georgios. I'd be satisfied in any life; so, I have often thought. For these few months, I saw my life with Deuc unfolding before me and I wanted to fashion it into a fine garment and wrap it around me.

Hear me on the shores of the issue. *Munan.* Deuc and I were lovers. To let someone come so close to you, to bond their life with yours, and create a connection between bodies — it is an obvious thing, and a dangerous one. Obvious, because we are all connected to everyone in this way. Dangerous, because most of the time we do not imagine it, but sex breaks that spell. Suddenly the thread is visible. Through my life, I have learned to follow my intuition and to devise which feelings indicate a path to tread and which ones to avoid. Seeing Deuc, I felt guilty. I was stealing a life path that was not mine. Neena knew when I spent the nights away from our cave or snuck in late.

"I don't think much of Deuc," she said, and in her Neena way made this sound as directed, but non-critical as possible. "I don't trust his intentions."

I struggled not to be defensive. A bad sign, I knew. "It was a brave thing for anyone to come down here."

"Sure, that, but it's a bit of an escape, regardless. Don't forget he sold us out to the pirates."

One night though, I came back and awoke to find Neena and all of her things gone.

When we met in the garden, I asked her where she'd gone.

"I've moved in with Haya and Tubal in the green quadrant," Neena said. "You should stop by and see the place."

Tubal worked in the object room restoring and caring for the metal pieces. The Mulians did not manufacture anything but cared for what they had. Haya worked on the friezes and murals that decorated the Mulian caverns. They had larger quarters, finely decorated, in the green quarter.

This time Neena was the one who looked sheepish and sounded defensive. She'd taken two Mulians as partners, joined their household, become part of a *munanhoma.* Tubal and Haya were respected artisans. Maybe in La Merde, if there had not been war, I would have found it odd in that society. On the Seastead, no one would have thought much of it. Here in Mu, we were all outside of the usual tenets of society. It made sense. Why should Neena be alone?

I was hurt that she'd left me, but relieved too. Our garden was becoming lush, our Mulian kelp was growing thick and high. We were melding into Mulian society. It was good to see Neena happy and it kept her from saying more about me and Deuc.

~ 16 ~

EGGS AND SKIN

The Mulians have many celebration nights, and Deuc and I were together on one of these in the darkest, coldest time of year, when it felt too cold to venture out into the sea, and there was a crispness and a frosted tang even to the warm *homa*. We were drinking an intoxicating Mulian mélange, their word for tea, and Deuc began to tell me his father's history. Balor's soldiers took the island Marshall was on, Corvo, and he was made to join them. He killed, but he was smart, and he saw a way to stop killing.

"I gave Balor the idea," Deuc confessed. "I said we should watch the Iron Bloods. He just wanted to get to La Merde. He thought he had relatives there. Some of the soldiers were friendly to me in town because of this. They gave me the contact with the Riptiders and I told them about the Seastead."

"You gave them the coordinates."

He nodded. I took a drink and digested this. I envisioned the Seastead overrun with Balor's men: Merl, Timbol, Georgios, and Desiree would all be killed or enslaved.

"So everyone we love up there is dead."

He shook his head. "I don't think so. I told him there was nothing worth taking out there, just a rusting hulk that wouldn't last. That you had some kind of serum, but it was faulty."

"Faulty."

"See, I told him the truth."

"You don't think Balor will have to see for himself?" Of course, he would.

"There are better places. There are legends that attract his curiosity: there's Noronha, the island of ascension, and Hiranya, the island of the sun. There are rumors of islands made of gold and of vast stretches of clear seas. Those will capture his imagination more than a pile of rust and some people he already let go. He'll seek those first."

"You don't think much of our Seastead."

"It isn't much. I know you have these hopes for it and ideas. But really, it's rusting metal, soon to sink like everything else. If we make it back up, we'll have to join the Riptiders on Elathe, if they'll have us."

"You're wrong," I said, speaking boldly in a way I hadn't to Deuc before. I sounded like the woman who had planned the Seastead again, not a Mulian farmer. "We have plans for a society and that's much harder than most people think. It isn't gold or mahogany or glory. It is a lot of dull meetings trying to get people to agree and communicate, but it's what can come of all that planning and meeting and organization and lists, see. It's like prayers. They seem like meaningless ritual, until they are answered. It just doesn't happen fast. You have to be patient."

I was talking to myself. When I looked up, Deuc was speaking also to himself. He was talking about his time on Elathe about the wooden planks, towers, and turrets. Our conversation had become a forked river.

"I told him a lot of things, not all the truth. On Corvo, he killed my sister. I don't wish him well. You would have thought he would remember that."

I caught the tail end of his diatribe.

"I'm sorry about your sister. Praise water. People only remember what they want to."

"Praise water," Deuc said, and he rarely did offer praise.

I understood what Deuc had done, his further betrayal, and what he had said. We spent the night together, but it was our last. In the morning, my mind clear, I knew I was done with him, repulsed by my weakness and for needing him to help me adjust to the strangeness of this Mu. Whatever intoxicating pheromones I breathed off Deuc's body had worn off. The sheen of him was scraped off my fantasy. I remembered that Deuc was here reporting for the Riptiders.

I gave Varuna the Whale a song for Georgios to warn him of Deuc's betrayal--a sad and warring song. There are no wind instruments, drums, or trumpets to convey the march forth of General Balor and send Georgios a proper warning. In whale song, war only sounds arrhythmic and desperate. I hoped Georgios understood.

I received a soothing reply. It was the first and last time I heard from Georgios in Mu. Varuna sang me the notes I have told her mean Georgios, my surface love. I knew it was a response to my song because I heard my notes repeated in it. I was comforted, but I had to be. There was nothing I could do except demand that the Mulians find a way to return me earlier. We were waiting for the return of the freshwater flute that could carry us to the surface. Perhaps, there was another way if I insisted. But what would that accomplish? I had to discover all I could about the Mulians. I could not go back to Georgios unchanged. I had to learn enough to be worthy of him so that we could never be parted again.

I imagined what I would do if I were on the surface and heard that General Balor could be approaching. I realized I would not be so alarmed. Balor had always been a possibility. Deuc's betrayal might hasten it, or not. Deuc was right. What does Balor want with a hunk of rusted metal? He wanted land. The Seastead would be a last resort for him. It was only the fellowships and actions of Neena, Georgios, Merl, Timbol, Desiree, and I that made the Seastead desirable.

At first, I missed Deuc's kisses and mourned them and his company, but my interest in him or any distraction waned. Deuc, Neena, and I grew fatter and sleeker like seals on the fruits of our own harvest and in the clean kelp-scented environment. Deuc and Neena made peace and began to compose music together. Deuc played the lute and Mulian instruments. Neena wrote the lyrics. For the first six months, we all looked fabulous. Soon, I felt gorgeous, plump, and soft. I wished Georgios could see me. After six months, I had acclimated to Mu.

I understood Mulian and felt comfortable. What a difference words made. Deuc and Neena took to playing at Mulian concerts and with a small band of musician artisans. I visited Neena sometimes in the green land in her new cave with Tubal and Haya. Their cave had many more objects and a more settled feel than mine. It was truly Mulian. We surfacers spent less time together than we had the first six months. Not knowing what Deuc was doing made me somewhat nervous. Was he seeing things I was missing? But I was glad to be free of him.

I was with the Mu for about nine months before I was allowed to see the room where the new Mu waited. The homa was beginning to become warm again and there was the faintest hint of lavender in the liquid around us. The rookery where the new Mu slept was deep underground by a hot spring rising from within the earth. It had a nutritious mineral smell like rising bread. It was a warm incubator where the Mu lay their young. I thought of the young as eggs, but this was not quite right. The Mulians called them Mua, which meant simply new Mu. I wished Timbol was with me to better help me understand the physiology. The rookery had a sleek gold coating and barnacles that rose from the floor like stalagmites with translucent pearl-shaped dome tops. Inside I could see moving gelatinous green, blue, and lavender threads. As they grew, they congealed and shrank, and they became gold coins embossed with tentacles stacked on the sides of the room.

"The Mua await the day when humanity fails and they can repopulate," Abrador said. "Some say it would be in our best interest to watch you fail. Some even say that we should hasten it. But I could not doom another civilization to our fate. It is cruel to be few and alone."

"You would rather help us," I said.

"So, it seems," he said. "We are ready to repopulate the earth, but it is not our desire to take over the world or to return to the surface. We have been hidden so long and have experienced peace. To return to the surface would be to accept responsibility, to intermingle and to admit, that this time, there is nothing in reserve. We 200 are all who are left. It is to mix and be changed and to possibly subject Mulians to war and passions again. It is to admit the end of our utopia in a new beginning."

In the eggs, I saw the Mulians' secret selves. I saw how fragile they were with those threadlike tentacles encased in gelatinous discs and how near to extinction. Still, it was not likely to happen, if ever, for hundreds of years, but the Mulians know, they can easily imagine, they can empathize with a species on the brink of survival.

"It is not your time, Abrador," I said.

He was easy to convince, as he did not want it to be time for the Mulians, yet.

"Then, if it not our time, you must *hovana*," he said.

I did not really understand the word, possibly some combination of transcendence and transformation, but it frightened me.

"I like myself as I am," I said.

"I like you, too. You misunderstand. *Hovana* does not mean to lose."

But his words, his careful words, did not calm me.

No long after this, I began to eat true Mulian mélange, which was thicker and savory and more than tea.

We had all avoided the slick food ever since we'd realized what it was made of: the skin the Mulians shed, cured and spiced. We'd had it on the first night but had not known what it was although it reminded me of the food Professor Belo had served us when she first brought the Seasteaders together at her party. If I had known what it was--peeled skin and the cells of immortality--I could not have imbibed it. According to legend, those who eat the skin become immortal. Yet, the Mulians held funerals.

"Those are the ones who choose to end," Abrador said. "The skin sheds as the spirit overtakes it and grows. The younger ones eat it. It is filled with a kind of oil that allows for immortality, secretions that cause longevity. It becomes thinner and thinner--the body, the skin, the corporeal self, until it dissipates.

One night the Mulian Council invited us to a special banquet. It was the hydrophoria feast almost a year to the day we had arrived.

"It's time for you to eat our food," Abrador said.

Of course, I ate their food, although I grew my own. He meant their skin.

Only Deuc refused. "I grow enough food," he said. He would stick to his own crops. He was not afraid of offending the Mu. He never was.

They invited me to feast, and it felt normal to eat the soup and it tasted so good, thick, oily, and spiced like a kelp curry. By now, I was used to the rubbery texture. The stewed mélange was the fattiest substance the Mulians ate. It was crisp and delicious. As a soup or tea, it left a thick oily smudge at the bottom of a cup or bowl and in a ring around the inside of the gold bowls and cups which then had to be carefully polished. Neena ate of it too, of course, but for her, I think, although she did not say, it was less of a change. I noticed that Abrador did not make a point of asking her to eat. There was a glow about her now and a lavender cast to her skin. I think she had been eating her Mulian partners' mélange for some time.

I was in the garden one afternoon, when I first became disturbed by the effect. I bent down and saw a splotch upon my skin, blight, like rust. After a while, I noticed changes to my skin, splotches of red rust color and hardness to the coating. My hair grew together and clumped. It was rusty and wiry. Neena looked different too, more traditionally Mulian, but also mottled with red. We, with our Iron Blood, began to rust.

"Did you know this would happen?" I asked Abrador.

"It's something different about your blood. We didn't know. Not exactly."

I began to cry, and my tears had a rust tint. They were light pink pearls of water. The tears always moved the Mulians to take pity on us surfacers.

"Come with me to the rookery. There's the first sign," he said.

We walked to the warm Mua cave, that hot sulphuric, yeasty room, where the eggs waited. His tentacles pointed towards the domed roof. I stared for the longest time uncomprehending. Abrador only waited for me to make the connection on my own. I heard the sound first a gentle plink, plink, plink. In the top, there was a pinprick of blue light, and it was dripping fresh water.

It was the beginning of our flute home.

"It's returning," he said. "And so will you in time."

We had about another year in Mu, but from this day, our return would be less than half the time we had already been away. I still remembered Georgios and loved him. From this day, my thoughts turned to home. Never, in my entire time in Mu did I think about staying. How different would my life had been if I had lived in that moment and settled among the people around me as Neena had? But I, I was always thinking of what I had left, and then of my return. In this regard, I was no help to the Mulians at all. I was not present.

At that time, as I began to change my skin, Abrador, was no help to me. I was horrified to see my way home now, horrified to see my rusting Mulian shedding, webbing hands. Now when I felt most monstrous, I began to face my return. How could I go home to Georgios like this?

~ 17 ~

THE RUINS

Now that I had seen that pinprick of light that promised my way home, I was obsessed with thoughts of return. Yet, there were many months until the flute would be large enough to transport us upward. We could not go in the bitterest cold either. We had to wait for the flute to form and the seas to warm.

We surfacers had gained comfort within our Mulian routines. We lived as the Mu lived growing our food, caring for our objects, and participating in music and ceremonies. The time would pass slowly now, too slowly, I thought.

Neena and I began to plan a trip out of Mu--not to the surface but to see more of Mulian society and the other Mulian enclaves. I had been out only on occasion to commune with Varuna but had stopped once I could rely on telepathy. Neena, however, had never been outside the confines of Mu into the sea. We wanted to see the ruins of the old civilization. The Mulians often spoke about Mount Meru.

Tubal and Haya had told Neena there was a festival when the enclaves gathered and made a processional to the ruins at Meru.

"They said they would take me then," she said.

"But doesn't that happen only once a decade?" I asked. The Mulians had a complicated calendar of festivals and rituals that I barely understood. "We'll be long gone by then."

"So, let's go now, just you and me." She wanted an adventure with me like when we had first arrived and met Varuna. I wanted that too.

Now that I could envision my homecoming, I was reluctant to leave and endure danger once again. I knew that it was dangerous in the sea among the predators outside of the Mulian dome. Still, there was a long time to wait until the water flute would be ready for our return and I wanted the time to pass quickly. I could not spend all my days waiting and thinking of Georgios. I found myself going to bed earlier and earlier, hurrying the days on.

The journey with Neena would provide a distraction. We intended to be gone many days. We'd swim through the ocean and go to the next Mulian enclave.

"Don't make the trip," Abrador said. "It's ill-advised."

In typical Mulian fashion, however, he was not convincing, and we knew we could do as we liked, make our own mistakes. We would not be dissuaded. Neena wanted some adventure, and we would never be in Mu again. This was our chance.

Neena came to stay with me as she had done those first weeks. We sat in the whirling, bubbling bathing pool together. We added some scented salts to it so that a lavender steam grew thick in the cave and watched the eye of Varuna the Whale through the dome. Then we put on our helmets, let the suckers attach to our faces, neck, and shoulders and dove down and swam out into the sea.

It was still quite cold and the *homa* was crisp and sweet reminding me of the inside of an apple. It made me tear up thinking of that surface fruit. The ocean was colder. I hated the chill and the openness and regretted being outside immediately, but I could hear Neena beside me. Our telepathic communication was strong.

Happy to be out with you. Adventuring!

She was joyous. She seemed much younger and freer than when we had first met. Her grief, although always with her, was less heavy upon her these days. She could remember Belo and smile. She could forget Belo at times as she enjoyed life without the consequence of guilt.

Varuna accompanied us through the ocean part of the way, but she did not like to stray from her grounds between Mu and the Seastead. We ventured West toward the other enclaves and the ruins at Mount Meru.

We managed to avoid sea predators. The other Mulian enclaves treated us kindly, but suspiciously. Mulians were not travelers, and they did not appreciate the concept. Travelers could not grow their own food or care properly for their objects. We had nothing with us.

Emptiness, the Mulians said. That's how our concept of traveling translated. Neena explained that her partners were caring for her objects while she was away. I had asked Deuc to take care of mine, but I could not imagine that he would place a high priority on polishing my tea set while I was gone. He never adopted or understood the Mulian view that those objects had souls.

The Mulians in the other enclaves treated us kindlier when we proved we could sing their songs, but they were difficult to understand and I realized what an effort the Mulians in our enclave made to slow their speech so that we could understand them even now after we had lived with them more than a year.

We made our way to the gold and silver pillared enclave closest to the dome, where we interrupted a festival of warming and fertility. The Mulians there were the most welcoming of any we had encountered. They were all drunk on a kind of mélange and soon got us intoxicated as well. They offered us strips of their mélange and sang louder when we accepted them. They were crisper, sweeter, and oilier than any other mélange we'd had. The strips dripped a viscous honey-like liquid.

Everyone was playing an instrument of some sort: bells, lyres, small drums or seashell castanets. The Mulian singers made slow liquid caroling sounds. They were singing of the past and the future, a beautiful, marvelous mix of images that became indistinguishable to us. The Mulians at this event moved in unusual ways, a kind of dancing. They shed their robes and displayed the barnacles and shells embedded in their skins. Tentacles and fins, thin and fine, thick and lumped, were all outstretched.

It was a fertility rite, one of the few times the Mulians copulated without an intent to produce eggs. I wondered if something similar was being celebrated back at our home and how Deuc would handle it. Well. He would handle it well, I imagined. Would Neena be sad she had not been there with her partners? She did not look sad now.

I wound up in a nook with a Mulian covered mostly with soft blue feathery tentacles and a dart-shaped tail. I observed how much my appearance had changed, but then I stopped observing for once and just enjoyed touch and telepathic communication. When the mélange wore off in the morning, I wound myself into those feathery tentacles again, just to prove to myself that it had not been a mistake.

The blue Mulian stayed with me.

"I can show you to the ruins," they said.

I found Neena. She only nodded at our feathery blue guide. I did not observe how she had spent the night. The last I knew was of everyone dancing with tentacles intertwined. Neena was never inclined to be judgmental and even less so now. We headed outside the enclave down a pebbled path, a carefully constructed shining path made by the Mulians for ceremonial purposes. When we could see the ruins ahead of us, pillars stuck into the side of a craggy underwater mountain flecked with gold. My blue tailed Mulian lover left us there.

"We Mu only go to the ruins at Meru, only for the ceremony," they said. "It is better not to disturb the *illisants.*"

"Illisants?" I asked Neena.

"Ghosts," she said. "My partners explained to me. The gold mountain, Meru, is where the ghosts live. It's where souls, who are not Mulian, wait to be reborn in the new Mu. The illisants wait in the objects that the Mulians tend."

We found Professor Belo's ghost, there. I remembered placing the Mulian coin, the Mua in her mouth. We did not see her, but she spoke to us. It nearly broke Neena's heart again.

"I made the water flute for you, in the Seastead, with that coin," she said.

I listened for my grandmother among the voices of the ghosts.

"Her blood was drained before her sea-fairing. She could not arrive here," Belo said.

It was another reason to abhor Balor. It stoked my hatred that he had taken grandmother from me again.

It drained Neena and I to meet with these ghosts and hear their tales of the afterlife.

"I see why the Mulians undertake this only with support, when they all go together," I said. "I see why Abrador warned us away from here. I don't like to feel so much hate and anger for my father, for the soldiers, for the Riptiders, and even Deuc. What will I do with it? It's so hard to tamp it down once rage rises within."

"That's war," Neena said. "Let it go."

It was easy to say.

We climbed to the pinnacle and looked down over Mulian society. There were twelve domes and glittering paths between them. Where we came from was the furthest East. There were many domes we had not entered. Looking up, real or imagined, we could almost see sunlight above coming from the surface.

We still had our necks craned back staring into the ocean when Neena said, "I'm not going back. I'm staying."

I laughed at first, not realizing she was serious, imaging she meant the ruins and then it dawned on me, she meant she would stay in Mu.

"Is it because of Belo?" I asked.

"No," she said. "I made my decision earlier. I want to live with Tubal and Haya. You can take the knowledge back. I'll stay here."

"But we'll need you." I meant on the Seastead where we all had our roles.

"It will be different," she said. "Besides, you never needed me. I was always extra, an aside to Alexandra's plan. I want to stay here with Alexandra and my new partners."

"You still miss her?"

"I miss her more. Every day there is something I could have shared with her. My sadness grows, but my grief lessens. I can handle it better, even as the tragedy becomes greater, because I see all the times together we have lost," Neena said.

"That makes sense."

"So, you agree? You won't fight me this time?" she asked, and I understood why she had wanted to make this journey with me. She still remembered how I made her leave the ferry dock at La Merde. She worried I would somehow be able to convince her to return.

"No, of course not, if the Mulians will let you, you can stay and with my acceptance. I won't try to sway you."

"The Mulians have already agreed," she said. "Look at me, Nata."

I looked at her carefully and noted her pliable lavender skin and clinging barnacles. She looked Mulian.

"I see. You've changed. Yes, stay. I won't try to convince you otherwise," I said.

"Good," she said. "Because you can be very convincing."

"I still have to go back," I said, imagining how I must look, Mulian and oceanic but also rusting and sloughing because of my Iron Blood.

"Nata," Neena said. "I believe you will. Listen. I've never been sorry I came with you to the Seastead."

Thank you. Love you. Appreciate you. She said telepathically. It struck me that those were the most important words, always the ones I had needed to hear. The ones I needed to say before I left everyone behind. Thank you. Love you. Appreciate you.

Neena and I returned to Mu through the dark cold waters. We watched the predators carefully and fended off any that came too near. Varuna greeted us when we arrived far enough East.

As soon as we returned, I went to the rookery to see the flute. It had opened wider and was the size of a fist.

I began to count the days and I went often to watch the progress of the water flute. Sometimes it seemed big enough I could slip my hips through, and other times shrunken so that it would pinch my waist, but still it grew. I calculated that it would be done earlier than they had told us. I pressed Abrador to tell me it was ready.

Finally, he said, "It will be ready soon...your flute home."

"Deuc and I can go now."

"If you want," he said. "Let us have a farewell ceremony. We have begun the preparations."

"Of course," I said. "We will miss you."

At the time, I wasn't sure I would. My thoughts were all for the surface and centered on Georgios. I longed for him now just as I had on the day I left, although I realized that much of what I had left of him and of my love was only memory.

~ 18 ~

FAREWELL

I imagine if I had not eaten the mélange or if my blood had been different, I would have remained beautiful and young in Mu. I could have changed my life for Deuc. I could have been a different person. It cannot be, of course, but I do love to imagine how Deuc and I would have stayed together in Mu. I would have taken up an instrument too, a Mulian flute, and we would have played together in the green, purple, and blue anemone covered Mulian fields. Imagine this life of contentment and love so different from the life I actually lived. This was a stream I did not follow.

Or imagine, Deuc and I, we could have gone to the surface together and then presented our finding about the Mulians to the Riptiders. Would they have taken us in as heroes or merely more useful slaves? Would we have known the difference? Could we have convinced ourselves otherwise, adapted to servitude so completely that we did not know differently? We would have been captives certainly and, in some way, I could have lived with that, rested with the Riptiders, without any responsibility and lived a simple life on someone else's craft that someone else was steering. It even seemed noble to me to do so rather than to always struggle selfishly after my own idea of perfection. Who was I to say what was best? But I did not let this tide pull me along either, and this outcome could not have been, because my blood would not let it be.

I ate the mélange and it changed me. It turned my skin to rust and wrinkles. With my monstrous visage, life with Deuc no longer seemed an option. I had chosen to eat the skin and be more of the Mu, and he had not. Deuc had not changed. Although he seemed more comfortable among the Mu than I, and he had made friends among the musicians, there was no question of him staying underwater.

When my skin changed, Deuc didn't treat me much differently, but he was spending more time with the Mulians. He was most often on the field trying out new rhythms and instruments with the younger Mu. Then, when I began to think more about going home, when it preoccupied my thoughts, I spent more time with Deuc. This time, there was nothing romantic. We were returning to the surface, and we were the only ones who shared this experience and that desire.

"Sometimes, I think, I wouldn't be sad to stay here, but then I remember," Deuc would say, "Sky, birds, wind, apples..." and he would go on and on like that listing all the things he missed from home until I joined him and added to his list.

"Berries, wood, velvet, ratfin...I miss In-fin." I told him about my life in the marshes of Salish Island. I told him about the feasts my mother prepared for us.

Neena joined us too, but not so often and she was silent.

"Would you ever stay?" I asked Deuc.

"Praise the mountaintop, no. Never. I know where I belong. This place, Mu, it doesn't make sense to me. It's so far underwater. It's too small and confined. Besides they don't want me."

It was true, the Mulians would not let him stay unless he ate mélange, and he would not. They did not want him to be alone. They did not want him to try to mate with their young Mu. Only, I think, because it would not work, and they needed the eggs. It was practical, not prejudicial.

"Would you?"

I was honest. "No, I got what I came for: understanding. I wanted to do this, but I'm for the surface."

"You want to be with Georgios."

"If he'll have me."

Deuc doesn't say anything, but in Mulian I hear him. *Of course.* There are no doubts for him. I wish I had such confidence, but one's own life must always seem uncertain. That's the drive to live. If we saw our own lives with the matter-of-factness that allows other people to see them, we would too easily be able to solve our own troubles.

And *become bored* by them, Deuc thought.

I did not agree. I was not bored by planning and slow progress. Building community, making relationships that would last, and seeing our work together wash over the years fascinated me endlessly.

With the decision made, and as time went on, I thought more of Georgios. When I'd arrived, I had thought of him every hour, I was composing letters to him in my thoughts that I was unable to send. I learned to compose songs instead. Then, as time went on, my hourly preoccupation with him, Georgios hovering ever in the back of my thoughts, began to fade. Instead, I thought of him daily or only when some new occurrence brought him to mind. Now, though, in preparation for the return, I thought of him on the hour again. I felt his presence as strongly as when I had left. I worried, however. Was it truly him I recalled? Or had I reinvented him in my imagination while I lived in Mu? Who was it I wished to return to? Was that person real?

Then, as the preparations for our sendoff became evident throughout Mu and going home became a certainty, I grew nervous about his reception of me. What was I going back to? Aged, crusted, and rusted as I was, I could not imagine a romance with Georgios. How would he see me now? I couldn't imagine how we would live together in the rust world. In the two years I had been below, we had been ages apart.

We had not been able to exchange words. We had exchanged only songs. I listened to the one song he had sent me over and over again and I read into it what I wanted until I was sure I knew him and his state of mind. Then not. I second-guessed myself and was uncertain all over again. Recently, there had been no songs at all.

The last song I sent him was titled "Homecoming." The words I meant for it were these: "My love, I miss you, I have missed you. My love, won't you welcome me home. My love, I am different than when I left you. You may never like to touch me again, but I love to touch you. In my mind, my skin becomes silken. I rust. I rust. Why have I suffered so without you? I know so much, but I am lost. Only let us be together again and maybe the future will become clear. Or won't matter. My love. My love. Mu send me home."

I wrote the words but knew he would hear only the notes from Varuna the Whale. I imagined he would know my meaning, but I hardly understood myself anymore. This song, more than any of the others I had sent, sounded the most like keening whale song. Maybe he would not even recognize me. Surely, I'd become too strange for him. I felt too strange for myself! But I wanted him. I'd spent too much time wanting him not to want him anymore. I was always one to stick to a plan.

On the day before our departure, the Mulians held a special ceremony for us. I went to it on my own. How well I knew my way around by then. I had no fear of the place, then great fear of it, and no fear again within the boundaries I knew. I looked around my cave-like room one last time with its walls, pearlescent as the inside of a shell, pearlescent as my changed skin. Inside Mu, as I have gone to rust, I have felt like an oyster, gelatinous, limbless, tough, liquid, and malleable. All of these. I ran my hand over the smooth, polished stones that ringed the pool where I often bathed and where I once dove into the portal to the sea. It's been a long time since I've been in the sea. It's safer inside, among the Mu, where I speak the language. I lifted the stones and peered into compartments filled with spices, foods, and objects. I take only my coral flute with me. I want to take the silver tea service, but it will be too impractical to swim with it and it would be wrong. The Mulians need these things. They love them. They do not have the capacity or desire to make more. These objects must be left to be cared for by a new Mulian.

I was sad to leave my water garden, which I had so carefully tended, and which fed me. I gave Neena the last of Desiree's tomato seeds. The nightshade grew well in the homa and larger and juicier in Mu than the vines ever would have in the rust air on the Seastead. If Neena harvested the seeds carefully, she could enjoy them for years to come. The Mulians, especially Neena's partners Tubal and Haya, were developing a taste for these surface fruits, too.

I wondered, would I miss the smell of kelp and cinnamon? I anticipated that I would miss the sound of the humming of the whirlpool and Varuna's cries. I would miss the Mulian music and the chorus of lyres and voices, all the sounds the community made when we celebrated and sang. I gazed up through the translucent ceiling and watched the shape of great Varuna the Whale glide overhead. She was so ominous at first. Then we became friends. I walked down the dark corridors of the living walls woven of kelp and covered with purple barnacles like jewels. The corridors were dark and intricate, but I knew them. I saw the phosphorescent markings directing the Mulians through the passageway. I remembered when I could not see them, and the hallways were like a maze.

The corridor emerged into the huge lawn, a mossy bed if looked at it closely, soft, and tumescent, a rolling lawn with small hills. The anemones were in bloom, and they covered the lawn in bright purple, green, and blue. They gave off a heady lavender scent. Already the music--harps, flutes, and chanting--had begun, I saw the council elders standing on a knoll before the coliseum and the 200 Mulians from all of the enclaves gathered round. I looked at their faces, their tentacles. This time of the year, there was a golden cast to their skin. I saw them. I felt them. I heard their minds. I knew nearly all of them by name. I looked up at their sky, which was not sky, but a translucent dome into the outside world. It had become sky to me. How much had changed in two years, I felt safe with them and loved them and this place.

The Mulians sang the songs of farewell and Neena and I ate the dish of mélange that contains some of everyone's skin. Even Deuc ate the dish this time. He would take some of them with him. It would make him live longer, perhaps forever. It was oily, thick, and delicious.

The homa around us felt light and sweet. I often shivered in Mu unused to the cold and the crispness, but on the last day of my leaving I felt comfortable.

"It is springtime above," Neena said.

The Mulians made presents of new robes for Deuc and I. They were long and sleek and sky-colored, a surface sky blue. We wore them and danced in the community circle so that everyone could see. The younger Mu teased Deuc. He showed them his naked torso underneath his robe. I was wearing a shift under my robe in preparation for the surface. The Mu gave me a packet of kelp and mélange tea. I wondered how long it would last me on the surface. They gave Neena gifts, too. For her it is not a farewell, but a welcoming celebration. A homecoming. She received more objects and instruments to care for, a sign of her acceptance. The Mu have not welcomed a permanent newcomer in ages. I saw Deuc watching her and imagined I detected jealousy in the look. Deuc always wanted to be loved most, the way the Mu loved Neena.

When we arrived, the Mulians had not welcomed a surfacer for decades. I knew that we would be legendary among the Mu and long remembered. If I were to return, even after hundreds of years, the Mu would call out, "Nata!" If any other surfacer were to arrive in Mu, the first question they would be asked, "Do you know Nata?"

I did not expect ever to return to Mu. Still, I could not believe I would be able to leave.

I enjoyed the celebration, but my thoughts were already surfacing.

I thought, just let me live long enough to leave this place. Just let me see home and the surface and the sun once again. Let Georgios hold me. I would have promised something, but I had nothing left to give. I had given up everything down to my skin, so I thought. I thought I had already made my great sacrifice for the world. I did not know that my two years in Mu were only the beginning of what the world would ask of me. What did I have left to sacrifice for the future I envisioned? Whatever it was, I would be asked to give it. And I would. I could not refuse that unknown future all of the gifts it required.

~ 19 ~

SURFACING

At that last celebration, I found my voice. I sang my desire to the Mulians. I sang of the surface. They stood and were briefly silent. Then they led Deuc and I in a procession down the lawn to the rookery. The elders left us at the entryway, for Mulians rarely enter the nursery unless it is time to procreate, an act unique from sexual intimacy (which occurs frequently and indiscriminately everywhere). Deuc and I descended the stone steps with Abrador as our guide again.

We entered the dark corridors and passed through the portico into the warm circular room filled with living orbs. I had not been so warm for some time except in the steeping pools. If Deuc and I had been Mulian lovers we would now kneel beside the eggs of pale lavender, blue, and green and sing until they broke open spilling a kelp plume into the viscous liquid of the room. Slender tentacles would rise out of the orbs and attach themselves to the front of our bodies and entangle us. The new Mu would be born out of our union and the souls of the Mu waiting in polished objects or from the souls of surfacers called from the ruins. They would be reborn. Neena would wait here hoping one day to be reunited with Professor Belo. Deuc and I could have lived another lifetime together in this way.

Instead, we looked up at the flute of water, a turquoise waterway back to the surface, and prepared for the journey home. Deuc put on a helmet again, but when I reached for one Abrador shook his head. Had it been that long since I'd looked in a mirror? I knew my face had become lumpy, but could I also now breathe water and withstand pressure differently?

By ingesting the mélange, I had become a sea creature. I did not need a helmet to breathe or to protect me from the pressure of the dank sea. This change embarrassed me. I did not want Deuc to know how complete my transformation had been. So, I took the helmet anyway and wore it although I did not need it. It was of no use to me, but I wanted it as a souvenir.

Deuc and I held hands when we stepped into the stream. It was instinctual, I think we both were frightened of what our return to the surface would mean for us. I could barely feel his fingers in the rusted webbing that had become my hand, but I was grateful he did not shrink from it, and I felt close to him. I could hear him telepathically.

Let us go.

We had come to rely on each other. I thought how I would never return to Mu and how I was grateful to leave. I was out of my element here, but I felt comfortable sometimes, too. I remembered descending to Mu in the water flute, how days passed coming down, and how we had the current with us.

To return, we must fight the flow of the flute to ascend.

It was light at first from the glowing dome of Mu surrounding its warm homa. When we passed through the deepest depths of ocean, it grew dark. We rose past the blackest depths of the ocean where the creatures shine with phosphorescent lights and bare sharp, glowing white teeth. We rose through the navy depths and closer to the aquamarine. We slept through some of the journey. We shut our eyes to pass the time. When the world around us had become teal blue with a sense of sunlight, Deuc, close by, got my attention. He held out his hand.

In his palm were two golden coins, spirits of the new Mu. They were not a gift.

Look what I stole, I heard him say.

The coins could be planted to create water flutes and purify the water. We could build more platforms and plant the seeds in the center. We could plant them off the shores of La Merde and live on the island's highest point with a fresh water source. That's what Georgios would want to do. He'd always loved the land. His attraction and need for it was not so strong that he would cling to it uselessly, to the point of death like his elders. However, land was a source of security for him. He would keep to the land, if he could. Those ways were not Deuc's. He preferred adventure to security. His purpose for the coins would be different--a bargaining tool. He would give them to the Riptiders. Deuc's theft saddened me, but it also held possibilities for us all I could not help but see.

Finally, we rose to where the light penetrated, and I could see the dried blood color of the rust ocean around us outside the cone of the flute. Rust sharks circled to snare the few stray fish that swam inside the flute and sometimes slipped free of the shelter of the freshwater cone. Deuc and I were careful to stay to the center of the flute as far from the toxic rust ocean and its mottled red sea creatures as possible.

The flute grew narrower as we rose, and Deuc and I kept further and further apart within it. We were remembering that we were at odds on the surface and perhaps even enemies. I felt his thoughts turning to the Riptiders, while I thought of the Seastead.

We were approaching the surface, and our battle of wills was beginning.

Riptiders, Deuc insisted.

Seasteaders, I responded.

An impulse.

A plan.

Freedom.

Collective action.

We heard each other plotting.

I hated that he had stolen the newborns. The Riptiders could not have them. I was making plans. I was already plotting against him.

Before I could surface, Deuc grabbed my foot. *No. Let's go back to Mu. Let's be together.*

We knew I had imagined we could break open eggs like Mulians together, he had likely heard my thoughts, but I could not believe he meant it.

The Mulians don't want you. People like you. Thieves. I was harsh and blunt.

He returned the favor. *You're too ugly for the surface, Nata. Georgios will gag when he sees you.*

We told each other hard, ugly, hurtful truths and approached the surface wounded.

Then, he grabbed my shoulders and pulled me down. He meant to drown us both. I struggled against him, but he was stronger. Finally, he pulled off my helmet. I surrendered, I feigned a struggle, but then grew still. I could still breathe, but Deuc did not know it. He did not know me very well after all. He had not really seen all I was capable of. But I knew.

Then Deuc threw off his helmet. He had no care for objects. He had not adopted the Mulian ways.

We will be reborn. It will be different.

He meant for us to die together. He preferred that end to being a traitor, at least. But I had already been transformed and I had my dream for the Seastead, for our utopia. I would not accept nothingness for either of us. When Deuc passed out from lack of oxygen, I pulled him to the surface. The sunlight was blinding, the air, moving about us felt wild, free, harsh, and frightening. It whipped and burned the surface of my skin and I gasped at the slice of it down my throat when I breathed the air again. My lungs pricked as if they were numb and waking. My chest captured all my attention as I struggled to breathe.

The surface was loud and moving frenetically: the waves, the wind. It roared. It blared. It frenzied.

The flute was in the middle of the ocean. It was a clear, clean pool surrounded by the darkest rust red sea I had ever seen. The corrosion had worsened. Rust sharks were swimming around the outside of the flute waiting to catch a fresh morsel.

I pulled Deuc to the surface and I tried to revive him, breathing for him, mouth to mouth, but I no longer had a mouth like that. I draped my face, my tentacles, over his and when I pulled back, I saw he was breathing again. My tentacles had saved him. When my eyes adjusted, I watched Deuc see me for the first time in the stark sunlight of the surface. I saw his horrified expression and then a more exaggerated version of the same meant for my benefit. I knew for certain now I was monstrous. I had changed more than I guessed. At the same time, I marveled at Deuc's beauty. His time in Mu had given his delicate features depth and polish. When his skin dried in the air, it shone like a stone plunged underwater.

I wanted him to live. Even if he was to be my enemy and would go to the Riptiders. What choice did I have? I reached for the packet of mélange and slipped some skin under his tongue, treading water with him in my arms, until he was able to speak.

"I was a spy," he said, the first words I had heard spoken in air for two years. The words leapt loudly out of his mouth and smacked against the surface of the sea. "One of Balor's men. I deserve my death."

Perhaps he did, as we all do, but I could not give it to him. I cradled Deuc, bobbing in ocean while I scouted our bearings. It was difficult to see at sea level, but I swam in circles within the shelter of the flute until I caught a shadow in the fading light. I saw a rust-colored strut rising. I edged closer to gauge the distance. The Seastead platform was about 500 yards away. I'd have to swim through the corrosion to get there.

After all the glittering, smooth, shine and curves of Mu, the sharp, dull Seastead struts looked ugly and unnatural. Deuc saw the Seastead too and he started for it. He pulled away from me and soon I saw the prehistoric shark fin lunging toward him. I swam out and grabbed his arm to pull him back, but I didn't see the other shark. The rust shark hit me, circled back, and tore along my arm and side with its rough hide.

Below, I saw Varuna the Whale's big eye. She had followed me to the surface and braved the corrosion again. I realized every time I had sent a message to Georgios, I had asked her plunge into the red rust. She sacrificed so I could sing to Georgios and be comforted. I swam through the corrosion and made for the whale. I expected the waters to burn, but I felt only fear. The sea was not even cold. Deuc's soft skin quickly became raw from the rust sea. He could not stay here. I gave him to Varuna.

Take him back, I sang.

I returned him to the sea as I had dropped my ratfin's corpse from the ferry, but I knew Deuc was alive.

His face tentacles attached to Varuna's side and she dove down with him. I sent Deuc back to Mu. I did not know what the Mulians would do with him. Varuna would tell them of his crimes. They didn't want him to stay forever as a member of their community, but I hoped now they would have no choice though they might well punish him for the theft and the betrayal. There were few transgressors in Mulian society. I did not know what form that punishment might take, but he would likely never see the sky again. Perhaps, that would be enough.

I thought of all the times Deuc and I had sat together in Mu and dreamed of the surface. I thought of what he had missed: the sky, the air, the quality of the sound, the apples and tomatoes. He was barely able to take a breath. He looked once at the sky before I sent him back. I betrayed him for utopia. My lover. My friend. My enemy.

I did not return the two new Mulians, he'd stolen, but kept them for myself. I did that.

I was alone. I swam to the Seastead and climbed up the metal ladder. I heard my clanging steps. Everything sounded louder on the surface. The wind felt sharp. The sun glared over the waves, beginning to set. It reddened the seas even more. The air moved and dried my skin. I had forgotten this and the strong smell of iron, the rust sea, the rust air, salt, and rotting fish. The salt stung my tongue and tentacles. The wind ran a harsh brush over my rusted appendages, and I saw the little red rust flakes flying around me, tiny pieces of my shedding skin, rust-tainted, airborne mélange. The platform looked like a husk.

The pool in the center of the Seastead was open and filled with thick, viscous rust sea. The Mulian flute had changed location. There was no source of fresh water for the Seastead now. No one was here.

"The Riptiders have taken them," I thought.

The Seastead looked old and empty. After life in the polished, swirling, purple-blue-green layers of Mu, the Seastead's metal struts looked faded, but there was a fresh layer of the brown dried-blood serum on it. If it hadn't been tended, it would have dissolved into the sea long ago.

I was shy at the thought of seeing Georgios, and I put on my long, formal robe--a gift from the Mulians. It covered most of my body from neck to toe. It was luxuriously soft. It protected me from the wind. I was a pillar of silver blue swirls. If I put my helmet on now, I would look entirely Mulian. Even without it, I was afraid I would be unrecognizable. All that remained of me were my very human clumps of hair. I wanted to make myself presentable, if not beautiful, for Georgios.

As the sun set, the floodlights came on. Then three people emerged from the kitchen. I could not hide in the shadows. They saw me fresh from Mu, after a long journey and a struggle, bedeviled with barnacles, disheveled from travel and fear.

I thought, *I love you Georgios. I do. I did anyway and I remember I love you.*

Then I let my mind become silent in fear and anticipation. My plans dissolved. There was nothing past the moment when Georgios emerged.

My love, my dear, my darling.

I remembered what it was like when I first saw the Mulians. I knew on sight that they were human, wise, and worthy of love although they looked so strange. I looked worse than they did. I was of Iron Blood, shriveled and red.

Later, when I saw myself in a mirror for the first time in years. It would be both better and worse than I thought. If I didn't think of myself as human, if didn't remember young Nata, it was better. My face was a collection of new lumps and textures, but my eyes were still my own, startled, and the whole effect was softer than I feared. Encrusted was not the right word after all. My face had been built up, but it was pliable and smooth in spots. Still, I could be terrifying at first glance. Imagine spinning around in air and coming face to face with a fish. It might be a beautiful fish, but unexpected. And I was not a beautiful specimen. Monstrous. Ugly. As Deuc had said.

When I first saw Georgios, I was stunned. I could not reassure him. I could not speak. I hummed. I sung my homecoming.

Georgios told me later, however, that he knew me immediately.

"You were humming that last song you sent me," he said. "Of course, I knew you."

I cried when he said that. Later, if I wanted to cry, I had only to remember, "Of course, I knew you."

Of course, he did.

We embraced and my rough, barnacled, finned arms scraped him. He pulled away and was gentler afterward when he lightly touched my arm. I was amazed that he wanted to touch me. Later, he told me he wanted nothing else. He loved me. He loved me still. It was a miracle. Once, I had wanted to save the world from the rust sea. Now all I wanted was Georgios.

Timbol and Desiree were also there. They were more cautious of me. Much had happened while I was away.

"Merl is with the Riptiders. We have a lot to tell you," Georgios said. "In-fin is here." He held out his arm and my now elderly ratfin walked down his arm to me, hid in my locks of hair, and curled around my rubbery neck as if he'd never left me. My dear lovely friend.

I watched Georgios and Desiree carefully. I remembered the song he had sent: wistful, romantic, and full of longing. Somehow, it had reminded me of Desiree's cooking and sensuality. I knew they had been together. I watched them still.

That night we played the game Cardinal as if no time had passed. It took me a while to remember it. The cards looked unfamiliar. Then I slid right back into the time when we had played every night. It was as if I had never left, except I fumbled a bit with the cards in my changed hands and I could feel the strangeness in my face when I smiled. Georgios looked as if he loved me still. Could it be by some miracle that he did? I stole sidelong glances at him from behind the cards. I drank the Mulian tea. I did not yet share it with the others.

"Where is Deuc?" Timbol asked.

"He stayed in Mu. I don't think he'll ever come back," I said. I had no idea how the Mulians would treat him. "Neena stayed too. She lives with a Mulian couple now."

I tried to tell them some of what Mu was like, but the words caught in my throat, and I became overwhelmed with remembering. I repeated the same words over and over: lavender, dome, stones, farming, singing, tentacles, barnacles, silver, ruins, tea, kelp, cinnamon. I felt they could not possibly understand. Yet, they were nodding.

After the game, Georgios and I went back to my room, which was left waiting for me untouched. I looked at my forgotten things. There were maps and fabrics that I had not seen for two years. I felt my youth return to me.

Georgios came close.

"You didn't look happy to see me."

"I am afraid."

"Why?"

I looked directly at him.

"You sent me all those songs and I sent one to you. Didn't you hear me?" he asked.

"I heard you," I said. "But I am different now."

He cradled my face in his hand. I was a child. I was a ratfin. I was his.

"I am so glad you are home," he said.

It was more than I had hoped for.

We were awkwardly together. It was not like the easy passion we used to have. I was uncomfortable and uncertain. But there was love, lust, and hope. We could be together again, even like this.

"There is so much I have to tell you," I said.

I knew I would never be able to tell it all at once. It would be years before I could explain what had happened, what it was like. The most difficult part of my journey had come. I was home, but I had to do everything I had delayed by my absence. I had to create the society in which we could live. There were so many rules to the surface life, and they all must be followed.

The first rule was war.

The islands war had continued in my absence and in the morning, with Georgios beside me--praise water, may he never be parted from me again--we heard the clunk of the ladder. There was no doubt who owned the ship alongside the platform. It was not a pirate galleon. It was not the Riptiders' Kyklopes. It was a vessel of war. The rust soldiers came aboard. I hid in the kitchen and listened. Who knew what they'd do to someone who looked like me. Timbol, Georgios, and Desiree greeted them. We anticipated takeover and madness. But it was not that.

The soldier who stepped forward was middle-aged. He had short sandy brown hair. Something in his carriage reminded me of my father.

"The old man. He just wants to come aboard. This is the last place he hasn't conquered."

"Then you leave," Georgios said.

"Then, we leave," he said.

I wanted to show myself, but I was afraid of these men who had been fighting too long, and would not see me for what I am, a peacemaker. So I stayed hidden.

General Balor came across the plank and boarded my Seastead.

He was an old man now and his breath came in thick, rasping heaves through wide open blue lips. He was sucking for air like a fish on land. He was dying.

I watched him all night and when the soldiers went to sleep, I sneaked out to sit beside him on the Seastead deck where he stayed in the open night air, the better to breathe. He had gone inside himself and my crooked visage meant nothing to him, but he could feel my peaceful presence. I held his hand in mine. I had the mélange with me, but I did not share it. I did not want him to live forever. I wanted him to feel peace and to be reborn with it. When the moon lowered, he took his last breath. I sung him to sleep, to death.

I could have saved him, with the tea perhaps, but it was not what the Mulians would have wanted. It was not what I wanted for this man who killed family and took my homeland. I felt better with him gone, relieved. On the Seastead, General Balor was given the sea burial denied my grandmother. His soul would dwell in the ruins of Mu as hers would not. Perhaps, his soul would return to us one day. I hoped he would have some memory of peace then.

Afterwards the soldiers lingered and made us doubt that they would leave as promised. Then they stripped the Seastead of any useable metal and stole the last of our Iron Blood serum. War was the first rule. The fight for land would continue until we were all gone and underwater.

I knew then what I had to do. I knew the rightness of the decision even while the weight of it settled into my stomach. It had the excited hum of a right choice instead of the heavy dread of a wrong one. I had learned to recognize this difference in Mu, and I would put it to use now. I could move forward confidently, even though it was the last thing I wanted to do.

I love you. I appreciate you. Thank you. May we never be separated again in this life or any other. I see you and, of course, I know you.

~ 20 ~

IRON BLOOD

That morning, the honor-bound soldiers left, but there was no doubt that they would come back with a new general. It was only a matter of time before the Riptiders came to find us and claim our blood for their serum and their safety from the sea. They would enslave the Iron Bloods. I didn't know what they would make of me.

I wanted to stay with my family--Georgios, Desiree, and Timbol--on the Seastead. I wished we could live in the peace I had planned for. I wish we had had more time, but I had to adapt to the new adventure and act on what I had learned.

After the soldiers left, I called my friends, my family, together. I showed them the new Mulians, the souls Deuc stole, the purifying coins we could use to stay together and have another life.

"That is what I want to do then," Georgios said, as I had expected.

Then there was a long silence as the others considered. It was as if were were at Cardinal again, everyone examining the cards in their hands and seeing the possible plays forward.

“There's another way,” Timbol said at last. “Not just for us four, but for everyone who is left.” He had seen it. The look on his face was grim and resolute.

"We can live in the sea," Desiree said, staring at my face and truly seeing me. “We can change like Nata has and become more

Mulian. We've been running from the rust sea, but we can make it ours."

I sighed with sadness but drew a breath in with relief. They saw the possibility, too. I was no longer alone.

"But the land," said Georgios.

"We can help purify the ocean again," I said.

"Once we are inside it," Desiree said.

Georgios looked from one of us to the other. He reached for our hands. "Yes," he said.

We talked long that night and for several weeks. It was not a hasty decision; true ones never are. While we thought, we played Cardinal, and I made love to Georgios and every time was ecstatic and likely one of the last. We did not drain blood to make more serum. The Seastead creaked and rocked, and we let it rust.

Finally, it was agreed. Georgios, Timbol, and Desiree began to drink the mélange every day and I taught them. When they had learned and their bodies had changed enough to welcome the sea and to be protected against it, we chose a day. It was the morning after a windstorm that shook the Seastead so the metal shrieked. We woke and saw bits of it had fallen off into the sea. There was a froth of rust corrosion around the platform.

It was falling apart. It was time to go. We said goodbye, and we sang each other songs, and finally we each dove into the sea and swam in a different direction. My family had become rusty, tentacled, and webbed like me. I went North, Georgios West, Desiree swam South, and Timbol headed to the East. I was not as sad as the last time I left Georgios. This time we were united in purpose. It was difficult to tell them I loved them when I was so afraid of death. Everything sounded ominous, like the last fearful goodbye.

But I had gone away and been reunited once. I knew that all these barriers between us; they do not exist. I knew that there was a strong chance that I would see Georgios again although it could be far away. I believed that when I saw him next, that time for certain there would be no reason for us to ever part again. I looked long into his eyes, the green pools, before we parted ways. No matter how he changed, I would recognize him: "I see you, of course, I know you."

Our plan, the Seasteaders' plan, was what it had always been, to survive in a beautiful, planned, considerate way. This time we would take to the water to find the many creative ways that people had managed to live outside of the water. We would offer those people our blood and the Mulian mélange, the skin of the Mulians and show them a way to live in the water and to swim forever. We would evolve back into the ocean of our ancestors.

Setting out across the sea in search of a settlement, I felt strong, as though I could swim forever, and had been, swimming forever. I undulated through the water fishlike and fast. My Mulian robe billowed around me. It looked like a cooling wrap over the burning red sea. I went alone, but also with the Seasteaders' plans and the Mulians' hope.

I swam for days before I reached a small peak. Long wood docks stretched out over the water. As I hauled myself out of the water, I noticed the scar where the Rust shark had brushed me in my conflict with Deuc. It had scraped away some of my rust hide. There was a slice across my side of beautiful, luminescent pale green, lavender, and blue pearlescent skin.

I saw hope that one day I'd shed the rust from my skin. When every islander left had learned to swim, I would be beautiful. Then, we could plant and spread the freshwater flutes.

We could never lower the water. We had lost the land forever, but the water could be clean again and fresh and we could learn to live within it.

While I swam in the rust sea, I felt the rhythm of one of Neena's poems. I sang one of Deuc's songs in my head. I heard the calls of whales. I remembered the Mulians. Although overwhelmed with my own survival, I would never forget them. One day, I would find a way to help them, too.

I considered the Mulians and how, while I was with them, Abrador and the elders had seemed so wise. However, Abrador was like me: different, focused on the future, and made odd and separate among the Mulians because he took an interest in the surface world (as I had taken interest in living on the sea).

The Mulians understood we were dying, but they were not wise deities above us. They were merely compassionate. They saw our days were limited as were theirs. They had compassion for our species, were benevolent, and desired to help. They placed a few Mulian coins in the way of a young girl. There was so much more they could have done, but they were afraid to act on their compassionate impulses. They were concerned with their own survival, and they were disorganized. They could not agree and plan and they needed to keep themselves secret for fear of being hurt. They didn't trust us. Most of us, I believe, would have been trustworthy. We could have helped more people faster if they had come forward. Professor Belo, myself, my grandmother, the people of La Merde, even those at Merops and the Riptiders would have helped, I think. Only General Balor and the men he poisoned would not...but maybe even they could have been convinced. If the Mulians had had the will and the courage. Maybe. It is difficult to tell, always, how goodwill, may be received. I could be wrong, maybe if the Mulians had taken more risk it would have been disastrous. I don’t know for sure what will happen next. I have only our hopes. I do know what I am doing now in this moment. I am swimming. We are all swimming.

We swam toward the islands where some people escaped the sea on the peaks. In a land of islands, many preferred isolation, what they were used to, and what they told themselves they wanted. The peakers wanted to stand apart. For them, we swam to each enclave and offered to share the gift of immortality and the ability to live in the sea. We would also share the music. We sang to them.

We must do this. We must act on our best impulses, this is what Georgios, Timbol, Desiree and I decided. Maybe we all had different motivations in a way. Timbol loved to explore. Georgios wanted to do what was right. Desiree sought to become something more and obtain a transformation. I was in love, and I felt if we succeeded, if we endured this one more fated task of separation, Georgios and I would be a certainty. I would have earned it. There was also, we all felt it, compassion for the world, the sea, and its people.

When I finally reached a landed place, the first people I met were afraid of me. I am a monstrous legend to them, a frightening myth. I swam on. The next place I stopped, there were a few people who joined me in the waters, and we received a visitor: a Mulian I did not know. He brought sad news. I saw him and immediately feared: What had happened to Georgios or Deuc? The first words I understood from the stranger: "He is dead."

But who? Which one of mine? They were at a loss to describe him. They described the similarities. Never had the brothers seemed so alike. It had never occurred to me how much they were alike, one and the same--not the physicality. The Mulian friend described their auras. These were nearly identical. For the first time, my tribe made sense to me. At that point in our lives, we were all shades of purple and white.

The light one. The light one. The one filled with light.

Finally, I knew who was meant. I began to cry, the salt tears that always endeared me to the Mulians.

I understood, Abrador had died.

He wanted me to know. He wanted to say thank you.

Thank you. I appreciate you. I love you. I see you and, of course, I know you for who you are.

That is all the stranger came so far to say. I remembered Abrador's reply when I said I thought the Mulians were helping us, "So it seems."

Were we not helping them in return? I had hoped Abrador would return. Would the Mulians come to claim their heritage on the surface of the sea? Were we not just preparing the way for them?

The Mulian messenger also left me a packet of mélange. It was a special brew that Abrador wanted me to have. It was made of his own skin. I shared it with the people on the island so that they would come to live with me forever in the sea. It tasted like sweet *homa* and tomatoes.

EPILOGUE

Here we return to the beginning. I begin my speech to this crowd of islanders as they look at my strange, red pearled skin.

When I returned from Mu the idea of being separated from Georgios and the Seasteaders again was unbearable, but I bore it. Now I'm bringing my experience and wisdom back from Mu and sharing it with all humanity.

The paths to Mu must remain hidden from the generals, soldiers, warriors, and Riptiders who would plunder them. The rule of peace must prevail.

After my speech, I swim on to the next enclave and the next. I no longer fear that my blood will lead me to an early demise.

I celebrate my 91st birthday. The older I become, the more Mulian I look and behave. I am silent except when I hum. My skin is leathery. It sheds in strips which I make into mélange. I am aging. I am evolving. I feed my mélange to In-fin.

In-fin, my long-lived ratfin friend, is my one concession to myself. I would not be alone and without a companion again. I taught him to swim beside me. I fed him my skin.

The next time, I crawl up out of the sea I am luminescent and beautiful, shiny, and clean, and I know I have an alluring strangeness. Now my task is made much easier.

The people will come to me faster lured by my hum and my song and enchanted by my luminous skin. They watch In-fin shake off his lacy wings and see his whiskers twitch. How will Georgios and the others be, younger than I, with their thick rust skins and oily coats? Will people recognize them for what they are? Salvation.

Someday, soon I hope to see Georgios again.

When next we go to Mu, when next we jump ship, we will go together.

Shel Graves is a reader, writer, and utopian thinker who lives by the Salish Sea. She is a solarpunk author published in the anthologies *Glass and Gardens: Solarpunk Summers* and *Glass and Gardens: Solarpunk Winters* from World Weaver Press edited by Sarena Ulibarri. Shel earned her MFA at Goddard College, Port Townsend, a utopia which no longer exists. Shel is an ordained animal chaplain with the Compassion Consortium and as Shel Graves Animal Consulting, www.shelgravesanimal.com, aims to create a culture of compassion and pay attention to animals.

May we all be confident, at ease, playful, and safe.

www.ingramcontent.com/pod-product-compliance
Lightning Source LLC
Chambersburg PA
CBHW060803310726
48980CB00002B/216
* 9 7 9 8 9 9 8 5 4 8 6 2 8 *